DECEIVED

ALIAS #4

LISA HUGHEY

Copyright February 2020

Lisa Hughey

Ebook ISBN: 978-1-950359-98-1

Print ISBN: 978-1-950359-07-3

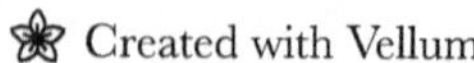 Created with Vellum

This is my twenty-fifth novel. That seems pretty crazy to me. This one is for my husband—and most importantly my partner—who brings me coffee in bed every morning and supports me unconditionally (even if he doesn't quite get what I do).

Chapter 1

"You need to steal the Rembrandt forgeries in the next two weeks before Christmas."

Ayesha Brown's heart stopped. She had spent the night at her grandparent's townhouse in their tony neighborhood after having a late dinner with her Gramps.

She paused at the base of the stairs, shamelessly eavesdropping on the conversation taking place around the corner in the library.

She didn't recognize the voice of the man who just spoke. He continued, "They're slated to be donated by the end of the year. You are the lead candidate to do the appraisal. I'm going to make sure they request you. Have the paintings disappear in transit or however you want as long as the theft isn't tied to me."

"I don't do that anymore." Gramps's voice quavered with tiredness and a hint of defiance.

"I don't care."

Who was this haughty fucker?

"You realize I'm too old for this?"

"You may be too old, but you've got to have contacts

who can do it for you. You were pretty old last time and managed to make it happen."

The voice was strong, imperious, and made Ayesha want to punch the guy, whoever he was, in the face. She took a quick peek around the corner and catalogued what she could.

White. Mid-fifties. Graying hair but styled and in perfect place. He had that whole "came over on the Mayflower WASP" vibe. But clearly beneath the innocuous appearance was human garbage.

"The paintings are at my father's estate on the Cape."

Cape Cod?

"They need to be stolen before they are discovered to be forgeries."

"What makes you think they'll be discovered?" Gramps asked.

"My fool father decided to donate the paintings to a museum, some lasting legacy bullshit. Even in death the old fucker is making my life difficult."

Ayesha wanted to snort.

Oh yes, it must be so demoralizing that your wealthy as fuck father didn't leave you all his million-dollar art. Your life is hell.

"Get it done or I will expose you to the authorities."

"I can just tell them who commissioned the fakes," Gramps said defiantly.

"You do that, and I'll make sure your son and daughter-in-law the ambassadors, and your granddaughter, pay the price for your disloyalty."

"You can't do that." But Gramps's voice trembled. Shit, he was getting old. And Gram's long drawn-out illness had taken its toll on them all. He was still recovering even though it had been almost a year since she passed. What kind of monster would threaten a man whose wife just died?

"Your precious granddaughter has a show coming up, doesn't she?"

If this guy knew her Gramps at all, he knew this was true. Gramps was super proud of her and shouted her burgeoning success to the rooftops.

"Leave Ayesha alone."

"If you don't want your family to pay the price, you'll get this done." The front door of the townhouse slammed shut.

Gramps had gone legit years ago. He consulted for the FBI and the Smithsonian and was an accredited and highly respected art appraiser.

Ayesha stepped from behind the wall. "Who was that?"

Gramps whirled around. "No one."

"Gramps."

"Jonathon Harrington the Fourth."

"Why does his name sound familiar?"

"He's on the board of one of the museums I consult for."

Okay. But that wasn't it. She cocked her head, fist on her hip, waiting for him to continue.

"His father was my mentor when I first started out in the restoration business. He's been to parties at the house."

"Was he talking about—"

"Don't worry about it. I've got it handled. I won't let him hurt you."

She didn't want to press. Her whole life she'd looked up to him.

Those forgeries couldn't be discovered. The shame and publicity would destroy her Gramps's hard-fought reputation in the art world. Every single appraisal he'd done would fall under scrutiny.

Warren Buffet had it right. It had taken her Gramps

twenty years to build his reputation but if this got out, it would only take five minutes to destroy it. Except for one time in her life, her grandfather had always protected her. He'd protect her again if this guy's threats were real. She refused to let this asshole destroy the man who'd raised her.

But…what the hell was she going to do?

Chapter 2

The road to redemption is paved with promises that must be kept—even at the expense of your soul. So here he was.

Marsh Adams was done. Done being lied to. Done rescuing people. Done being duped by women, or even worse, and more importantly, the most consequential liar of all, his father.

He didn't want to be here.

But he'd promised his business partner, and his mother, that he would see what the judge wanted. He had a lot to atone for in the past four months, so even though he didn't want to be here, he would keep his promises.

He walked into Judge Robert "Call Me Bobby" Adams's office with its ornate old-fashioned wood panel wainscoting, stately evergreen walls, and brass lamps pouring shadowed light over his father's very important work. The first step inside was always bittersweet. The slight overlay of lemon furniture polish was accompanied by that burst of pleasure, and then remembrance set in and the smell turned his stomach.

His father's office had represented happiness, love, reverence. Until it hadn't.

Marsh had walked in on his father and an aide, a girl in her young twenties, a law school student. And in stunned disbelief watched his father pounding into the young woman's willing body. That moment had changed his life forever. The betrayal of his mother, the betrayal of their family, the betrayal of his ideal of his father, in living technicolor, had gutted him. And destroyed their family.

That moment was embedded in his psyche. Now every time he walked into his father's office, he relived it. Over twenty years had passed. But he had never forgiven his father. He never would. And every time he walked into this office, he remembered with shame that once upon a time he had adored his father. Had wanted to be everything like him. Wanted to be him.

Marsh had spent the rest of his life attempting not to be like his father. And yet, in his zeal he was afraid he had become just like his old man.

"Good morning," said the attractive young woman guarding the hallowed—tainted—halls of his father's office.

Someone new. Marsh rolled his eyes. Fresh meat, just his father's type. "I'm here to see the judge."

"Do you have an appointment?" She smiled quizzically. She had no idea who he was. That pretty much summed up his relationship with his father.

"Marsh Adams."

Her red-painted lips formed a surprised O. "Oh yes. I see he blocked out the time. Umm…" She clicked on her computer screen and then smiled with embarrassment. "He's got someone with him right now."

"Don't worry. I know the way."

"Let me just check—"

"Sure." He waved his hand and strode toward his father's office door, basically ignoring her. He knew was being a dick, but he wanted to get this over with.

He paused at the door to his father's inner chambers and smoothed a hand down his paisley silk tie. Shook the shoulders of his traditional navy pinstripe suit to get the lines to fall properly. He had wanted to come in jeans and a sweatshirt. But he'd promised his mother. And his business partner Jillian. He had also promised Jillian that he would share with her everything the judge requested.

Their private witness security and witness relocation business, started after they left the US Marshals, had taken a hit when Marsh had trusted a client, ignoring red flags and warning signs because he was attracted to her, and she had duped them all.

Then he'd screwed up even further by not trusting Jill and attempting to fix his mistake all on his own. Instead he'd almost cost Jill her life and he'd irreparably, fundamentally changed their relationship and damaged the credibility of their business. Previously they had managed to keep under the radar by presenting a front as a public relations firm and hiding their clients' identities from everyone. But now the business was under scrutiny by law enforcement and they were all trying to do damage control and clean up his mistakes.

Things in the office were back to normal. In theory. Except Marsh no longer felt comfortable in his own space. He hated that he had let everyone at Adams-Larsen down. His partner and his employees, his friends really, no longer trusted him. Frankly, he didn't trust himself.

Everywhere he went, he felt just slightly out of step. As if he no longer fit in his own skin. As if the taint of Brianna Walsh had wrapped him in a film. Everything looked the same, but *he* was different. And he couldn't seem to get back to that comfortable camaraderie with his friends and employees that he had taken for granted before.

Everywhere he went, the feeling of other, of strangeness hit him. An alien-ness that wasn't going away. No matter how much he pretended that everything was fine, good, normal, it wasn't.

Even his father's office felt off.

Marsh had been taken in by a sexy, gorgeous face, and an entire cadre of lies.

He was done being lied to. And, he was done rescuing people.

Marsh rapped decisively on the wood door, his knuckles abused by the last sharp knock, and paused for the requisite seconds, waiting in case the judge was in a compromising position.

His stomach tightened and his gut clenched. Every time he came to his father's office, he remembered the day that changed their family forever.

After an appropriate amount of time, he pushed open the door, expecting to see the judge and another clone of the receptionist smoothing away signs of a liaison. It was a wonder the randy old bastard ever got any work done.

Instead of a sexy young thing, an older Black gentleman sat in one of the chairs across from the judge's massive— overcompensating much?—desk.

"Marsh, my boy." The judge pushed out of his chair and headed toward him. His pima cotton dress shirt was rolled up at the sleeves. This guy must be a friend, because the judge didn't get casual in front of many people. Appearances must be kept up.

The judge wrapped his arm around Marsh's shoulder, and the scent of English Leather hit him.

He sidestepped the weird attempt at a hug and gave his father a curt nod. "Judge."

The judge cleared his throat as the dapper-dressed man rose to his feet gingerly, moving as if his body no longer worked for him and he had to fight for every motion. A giant smile wreathed the man's face. The dark skin around his eyes crinkled, and his thick salt-and-pepper eyebrows rose, his deep mahogany eyes sparkling with pleasure.

"It's about damn time." The older man reached out his hand, his gnarled knuckles swollen with arthritis, and clasped Marsh's hand in his. His other palm bracketed his hand as the old man squeezed gently. "It's a pleasure to finally meet Bobby and Colleen's son."

He certainly had Marsh at a disadvantage.

"This is my old friend, Lincoln Brown." The judge clapped Lincoln on his shoulder. Marsh catalogued details as the old man stared at him. Bespoke tailored suit, likely London-based, vest with an antique pocket watch bulging from the pocket, the chain looping across his barrel chest. Italian loafers, slip on, likely because the man's arthritis made it difficult for fine motor dexterity.

He clearly had the money to color his short graying afro but chose not to.

Lincoln Brown. Marsh had nothing. The name meant nothing. But Lincoln Brown certainly seemed to know who Marsh was. "Nice to meet you, sir."

"No need to stand on formality, son." Lincoln Brown shuffled back to the chair and sat down carefully. "Call me Linc."

"Have a seat, have a seat." The judge gestured to the chair next to Lincoln Brown.

Marsh sat as the judge returned to his seat behind the desk. For a second, Marsh studied his father. When had the old man gotten so *old*? True, he had avoided the judge as much as possible over the past few years. But there was an odd fragility to him.

"Good to see you again, I thought for a while that maybe you weren't coming back."

Marsh fought the urge to shift uncomfortably. The truth was he had disappeared. That was pretty much the entire reason he was here right now. Because he had promised. Both his mother and Jillian.

"Just busy." Marsh let the silence build. The room was heavy with oppression and disapproval. His father had called him here but now wasn't forthcoming about why. When no one said another word, finally, he had had enough. Yes, he'd promised but this apparently wasn't anything urgent. "Well, since you're busy—"

The door swung open with a crash. "Sorry I'm late." A slender Black woman swept in like a tropical storm.

His first impression was color.

Bright, vibrant movement. Whirling dervish. And color.

He started at the bottom and surveyed his way up.

Worn, pale blue Converse high-tops splattered with paint. Ripped skinny jeans with splotches of paint in bold red, yellow, bright blue, even some neon green and orange. A white tunic sweater slipped off one shoulder revealing bare skin and collarbones. The nipples of her small breasts pushed against the top, boldly proclaiming her braless.

Her face was stunning: high cheekbones, regal nose, black arched brows. Striking hazel eyes shimmered with secrets and mirth, as if she had a private joke just for them.

Except everyone probably felt like that around her.

She was one of those people who oozed magnetism and sex appeal.

Just like his father, if he were honest. And that thought

made him want to gag and then spew all over the old man's office.

She had skin the color of rich Brazilian hardwood and hair a natural halo around her face. She had another splotch of paint on her bare neck, and her fingers were long and elegant and adorned with paint, as she gestured at the old men. "Problem on the metro. Was stuck on the train."

Everything about her screamed free spirit and unrestrained joy.

"Ayesha, darling." The judge walked toward her with open arms and embraced her. He squeezed her tightly, just a little too long. But in an odd turn of events, Marsh didn't think his father's touch was sexual. He seemed almost paternal.

That was weird.

"Good to see you again as well, Uncle Bobby."

"Lovely to see you again, my dear." His father slung his arm over the woman's shoulder and turned her to face Marsh. "This is my son, Marsh."

Uncle Bobby? Now Marsh was really confused.

"Marsh, I want you to help Ayesha."

What the hell?

AYESHA BROWN STOPPED in her tracks. Raised one eyebrow and scanned her gaze over Marsh Adams.

So *this* was Marsh Adams.

She'd been hearing about the prodigal son for years, but she'd never met him.

He was…not what she expected. Oh, he looked a little bit like his father, taller, thinner, with his paternity written in the austere lines of his pale white face. She tilted her head and studied the angles of his face—he had the square jaw and high forehead that emphasized his eyes, but his nose was crooked, adding interest to the otherwise perfect lines. Peripherally she noted his clothes, appreciating the suit porn.

Pinstripes. Tie. Shiny shoes. Stuffy. Tightly wound. Buttoned up. But that nose didn't fit with the rest of his appearance.

Since she knew how much heartache he had caused his father, she nodded once at him and stuffed her hands in her pockets. A clear rejection of cultural normative standards. She wasn't about to shake his hand.

"Sit down, sit down."

What on earth could this meeting be about? She had bigger things on her mind than meeting one absent and neglectful man child. Her first big show was coming up right before Christmas and she still had pieces to finish. Worry gnawed at her stomach because even that paled next to the other even bigger—gargantuan even—problem. What to do about Harrington and his demands.

She'd done some research on the guy. He was connected, wealthy, and by all accounts an upstanding citizen.

She shot a quick glance at her Gramps. He looked better than he had at breakfast after that asshole had threatened him.

Despair tried to roll through her. But she shoved it back with the hard-knuckled fist clenched in her pocket.

The truth was she couldn't let anything happen to her hands right now so she purposefully let them relax.

Marsh Adams's gaze shifted to her hands. As if he noticed her frustration.

She would bet this guy didn't miss much.

She sank onto the chair and perched on the edge, pretty much ready to bolt as soon as this—whatever it was —was over.

"Marsh's agency can help you out," the judge said.

His agency? Last she knew he ran a public relations firm in DC with a partner. Before that he'd been in some sort of law enforcement.

"Public relations?" Now that she could get behind. She needed this show to be a success. For that, she would put aside her disdain for Uncle Bobby's son and work with him.

"What problem do you need to make go away?" Marsh asked.

"I don't have a problem."

The implication that she had problems annoyed her. Marsh scanned down her body again. Everything tingled. She would not be attracted to this asshole. And she knew just how to get rid of him. "Why is it that white folk always assume we Black folk have a problem?"

"I didn't assume anything." He smoothed his hand over his tie. "But most of our clients—" there was a weird emphasis on *clients* "—are in trouble and they come to us to smooth things over." His voice was even, unemotional.

Curiosity got the better of her. "Who are some of your clients?"

"I'm not at liberty to discuss that."

Snooty. Jesus, this guy rubbed her the wrong way.

Gramps interrupted. "Ayesha is an artist." Pride was evident in his smile and the crinkle around his eyes.

"She has a show coming up in a few weeks." The judge pressed his hands flat on his desk blotter. "I was hoping you could give her the friends and family discount."

Marsh Adams looked like he had about as much understanding of what that meant as she did.

But for a moment, hope buoyed. The gallery that was putting on her showing was cutting-edge but new and not yet established in the high-end art market. Any publicity boost from his firm would be welcome.

"I…."

Clearly he didn't want to help her out and he'd been ambushed by two old fools—who she loved—but she didn't have the patience to play the ego-boosting game today.

"It's fine." Ayesha stood, resting on the balls of her feet. She couldn't wait to get out of here. "I don't need a PR hack."

"Hack?" Now he was starting to get riled. "We aren't hacks."

"Not so fast, my dear." The judge shot a censuring look at Marsh. "That's not actually what I was talking about… although it isn't a bad idea. Maybe you can get Jillian on the promotion for her art show."

Gramps said, "I told Bobby about our problem."

Ayesha jolted. Pure terror slammed into her. He had told the judge? About the threat to their family? What that asshole wanted Gramps to do was illegal. He couldn't have possibly shared that with a man sworn to uphold the law. That couldn't be right. And what the hell could a PR guy do about their family issues? Family came first. And as much as "Uncle" Bobby was Gramps's friend, cluing him in to their potentially larcenous behavior was a bad, bad idea.

The slight smirk on Marsh Adams face had disappeared. "What problem?" His body hummed with a latent energy.

"Someone threatened her," the judge said.

Ayesha relaxed. That was what her Gramps told the judge?

"It's nothing." She smiled tightly and shook her head.

Gramps's hand shook as he patted Marsh's. "It's not nothing."

"She needs a bodyguard." Uncle Bobby pointed his finger at Marsh as if appointing him as her protector.

What?

"No, I don't," she said at the exact same time that Marsh Adams said, "Not interested."

Chapter 3

The shock on Marsh Adams's face was priceless.

Mr. God's gift to whatever was stunned that she turned him down. The last thing she needed was a bodyguard. She wasn't going to let Harrington the Fourth, asshole and morally corrupt guy, destroy her grandfather's life. However she decided to handle it, she couldn't do anything with an audience.

"Well this is been…enlightening." Ayesha let her amusement show and stood quickly. She squeezed her Gramps in a hug just a little too tightly. "But I've got to get going. Those canvases won't paint themselves."

She bussed Uncle Bobby on the cheek and then headed for the door. Marsh Adams meanwhile stood completely still, rooted to the floor, and studied her.

His intense regard was almost like a physical caress, and again she wished that she could paint his face. For someone who gave the appearance of being impassive, he practically seethed with emotion.

Ayesha headed for the exit, more than ready to get out of here. She strode down the hallway, her shoes sinking into the plush deep carpeting. She grabbed her wool winter coat from the hook outside the door and wrapped it over her arm. She was a tad overheated at the moment, so she'd put it on later.

But as she reached the exit in the receptionist's area a hand on the door halted her hasty retreat.

She hadn't even heard him move. His big body should have made that impossible.

"A moment, please."

Ayesha studied his white hand, broad fingers, blunt-tipped nails. A strong hand. His blue veins popped, leading to a sturdy wrist revealed as the cuff of his shirt strained against his forearm.

The narrow distance between them was in no way intrusive, and still she felt crowded, caged in, which was ridiculous, but somehow that didn't matter.

Ayesha turned around and leaned back against the heavy wood door. She tilted her hips and crossed one foot over the other. The pose casual, cocky. But she held her coat against her waist, the wool a flimsy barrier between them.

She canted her head and looked up at him through her lashes. "I don't think so."

Again, she had shocked him. "What?"

"I don't think we have anything to say to each other."

"I just want to make sure that everything is okay."

"Why? We don't know each other."

"Is your grandfather prone to drama?"

She bristled. He could be ticked at her all he wanted but he better not criticize her Gramps. "Of course not."

"Then why does he think you need a bodyguard?"

"Why don't you run along and ask him?" Ayesha was done. "I have things to do. And I don't need a bodyguard, thanks." Where "thanks" totally meant "fuck off."

Instead of getting him to go away, he looked intrigued. She stared pointedly at his hand keeping the door shut. He grimaced. "I guess I will leave you to it."

Disappointment fluttered in her belly but she didn't know why. He was doing what she wanted.

MARSH STRODE BACK into his father's office. The two old men were huddled over the judge's desk conferring. When he slammed the door, they broke apart as if guilty. "What is really going on here?"

"I'm just worried about my granddaughter." Lincoln Brown looked at him with sad eyes.

"Why?"

"It doesn't matter. We will figure out something else."

This whole setup stank. Something was going on. There had been a moment when he'd been talking to Ayesha and fear had flashed in her defiant gaze.

He felt compelled to explain. "If she refuses services, there isn't anything I can do."

"What do you care? You turned me down—let me down—anyway." The disappointment in his father's gaze pissed him off. Who was Bobby Adams to be disappointed in him?

"Yeah, well, now you know how it feels."

Marsh was done.

But shit, he couldn't get that glimmer of fear out of his mind. She was brash and cocky and full of attitude. Fear didn't even figure into his assessment of her. Until that moment by the door.

Marsh couldn't get over Ayesha Brown's attitude, so he was going to do something he shouldn't.

He followed her. She took the Metro. He kept far

enough behind her and she was sufficiently oblivious that he was able to tail her without any problems. If there was something wrong, if she was in danger, she ought to have better situational awareness. The fact that she didn't caused an anxiousness in his chest. He shouldn't care, and yet he couldn't stop himself. That protector gene was ingrained deeply.

He followed her to Indoor Parkour, a local parkour course. She stowed her bag in a locker and turned toward the advanced indoor course.

She appeared to be totally engrossed in whatever was on her mind, leaping and rolling, darting and dashing through the course with an agility that indicated this was a regular activity for her.

He could admit to being intrigued. She was an artist and the very athletic, training-intensive activity seemed at odds with her appearance.

However, when he thought back to her sexiness, to the way she moved with a lazy grace, he realized the hobby fit her perfectly.

Marsh stayed in the shadows, watching until she was done, then followed her again. While he kept an eye on her, he dug into her background, pulling up basic information on his cell. When she got on a Metro line that would take her to the neighborhood she lived in, Marsh let her go.

He headed back to the office. His reason for living. He had a promise to make good on.

"HOW DID it go with the judge?" Jillian Larsen, his business partner and friend, poured a cup of coffee from their office communal pot in the conference room—formerly the dining room of the old brownstone they'd renovated into a kickass office when they'd started ALIAS.

"Strangely." Marsh picked up a sugar cookie in the shape of a Christmas ornament, decorated with thick, colorful frosting.

"You're stalling." Jill sipped her coffee from a mug that said *La Jefa*. The boss in Spanish. Even though they rarely saw clients in the office, she was always dressed in her business best. With her white blond hair smoothed into a tight twist, red lipstick in her otherwise pale face, and a suit that wouldn't look out of place at the Capitol, she was the ultimate lady boss in a pencil skirt and pumps.

"He wanted me to be a bodyguard."

Jill stopped. "For who?"

"For a friend whose granddaughter needs protection."

"Who's the friend?"

And that's who he should be researching: Lincoln Brown. It all started with him. "Lincoln Brown."

"The art appraiser and FBI consultant?"

Well, that made things more interesting. Lincoln Brown was an art appraiser and consultant to the FBI? Why wouldn't Brown just ask one of his Fed acquaintances if he was truly worried about his granddaughter?

"I guess so." But Marsh was done rescuing damsels in distress. "I told him no."

"Do you think there's more to it?" Jill's lips quirked. "After all, with Bobby Adams, there's usually some spin you weren't expecting."

"That's for damn sure." The instinctive disdain for his father hit him in the stomach. He shoved it down, determined to make Jill understand that ALIAS came first. "But it doesn't matter, she didn't want a bodyguard."

They headed up the grand staircase toward the suite of executive offices. "Interesting."

But that glimmer of fear in Ayesha Brown's eyes wouldn't leave him alone.

"You think there's something there?"

"I don't know." Clearly his intuition was skewed. Marsh followed Jillian into her office. This was the room where they met with their clients.

Jillian placed her fingers on his forearm.

"But I'm not about to waste company resources on a nonstarter."

"Marsh, your instincts are good," she said reluctantly. She'd said she'd forgiven him for the debacle with Brianna Walsh but there was a distance in their relationship that hadn't been there before.

And were his instincts really that good? He'd been taken in by a con artist. Sure, he'd tried to remedy his mistake, but Adams-Larsen was still paying for his lapse in judgment.

"Something seemed off."

Jill laughed, her eyes lit up with amusement. "Isn't that pretty much par for the course with your father?"

She'd been laughing a lot more these days. "The Scottish bastard has been good for you."

"Yes, he has." Jill paused. "Do some research on the granddaughter. There's got to be a reason that Bobby wants a bodyguard for her."

He said fiercely, "I won't do anything to jeopardize ALIAS."

"I know."

But Marsh wasn't sure she believed him. For what it was worth, he wasn't sure he believed himself.

"Hey." Kita Kim, his high school pal and now coworker at ALIAS, plowed into Jill's office and threw herself onto the love seat. Her straight black hair was pulled up into a messy ponytail showing the high cheekbones and tilted black eyes of her mixed Vietnamese, Chinese, and Scottish heritage. "How'd it go with your dad?"

"Make yourself at home," Jill said drily.

Kita laughed, then made a "get on with it" gesture at Marsh. He liked seeing the easy camaraderie between his two favorite women in the world, beyond his mother of course. Before he'd disappeared, they'd been more wary around each other. But they had bonded while he'd been gone.

Marsh went through the details of the meeting again.

"She turned you down flat?" Kita hooted with laughter. "Bet that was tough for your ego to handle."

Was he really that transparent? Did he have some weird need to rescue women? And hadn't he just resolved to quit?

"Speaking of your parents…." Kita butted into his mental wanderings. She looked at Jill. "Have you talked to him yet?"

"Talked to me about what?"

"You really need to…have a talk with your mom."

Now both women were looking at him in a way that was freaking him out. "Is everything okay with her?"

"There's just some stuff that came up during the case when Kita met Alex," Jill said.

"What kind of stuff?"

"Personal. Stuff," Kita said.

Now he was really freaked out. "She doesn't have cancer or anything, does she?"

"Your mother loves you."

Well that wasn't making him feel any better. Kita squeezed him around the waist in a one-armed hug. "Sometimes it's hard to see our parents as adults."

Now he was really confused. Her father had died when she was young, and she and her mother were estranged. For extremely good reason. And Marsh knew for a fact that Kita thought of his mother as her surrogate mom.

Jillian's mother had taken off when she was a baby and her father had disowned her after her fall from grace at the US Marshals.

"Neither one of you deals with your parents as adults."

Kita and Jill both winced.

"Maybe we should tell him first," Jill said, glancing between the two of them.

"Tell me what?"

Kita rubbed at the bump on her wrist. "You might be right."

"You may want to sit down." Jill gestured to the seating area.

Marsh settled on the small love seat, Kita on his left and Jill in the wing chair on his right, the wall of books behind him pressed down on him. "Please just spit it out. Whatever I'm imagining can't be worse than the truth."

Kita muttered, "You can't imagine this."

"Guys—"

"Your mom…and your dad have a thing," Kita blurted out.

"A thing? Course, they had a thing. They had me."

Kita squirmed in her seat. Have. A thing. Wait.

"A long time ago."

"Actually, not just a long time ago." Jill's hand fluttered as if she was going to touch him and then decided against it.

His brain froze. His heart froze. "Umm…are we talking about…?" He couldn't even bear to say it.

"A sex thing," Kita said.

"That's impossible."

Jillian shook her head ruefully. "Apparently not."

"How do you know this?" Not that he was admitting that this was a thing. But still.

"When the judge was getting his threatening letters, we had to look into all of his…liaisons," Jill said gently.

"Let's not candy coat it. His affairs," Marsh said harshly.

"Can it be it really be called an affair if you're not married?" Kita murmured.

"Splitting hairs, Kita," Jill said.

"Point taken." Kita sat up straight. "Let's just say your father is extremely active."

"So my mother, and my father…" He couldn't even bear to say it. He shuddered.

"Once a month," Kita said. "At the Hay-Adams."

"Jesus." He didn't even want to think about that. He covered his eyes with his hand as if he could shut out the visual. "Too much information."

"Yeah, sorry," Kita said.

"But why?" He couldn't fathom it. His father's infidelity had torn apart their family.

"I would suggest you talk to your mother about that," Jill said.

"Yeah, I guess I will." But shit, his mother should not have anything to do with his father. "Clearly, we need to have a talk. She needs to understand that this is not okay."

Jillian laughed. "Marsh, she's your mother, but she's not dead."

"I get that." Ugh of course he did, but he certainly didn't want to think about his mother as a sexual being. "But with my *father*?"

"Yeah." Kita put her head in her hands. "That was not a fun conversation."

"Which one?"

"Either or both." Now Kita was the one with her hand over her eyes.

"You talked to my mother about this?"

Kita flushed. "We had to interview everyone with an intimate connection to your father."

"That must have been horrible."

Kita said, "Actually even worse was when I found out he'd been sleeping with my mother too."

What?

––––––––––––––––––––––––––––––––

Chapter 4

––––––––––––––––––––––––––––––––

Like a creeper, Marsh sat in his car outside the funky loft in a questionable neighborhood. Gentrifying. Probably not the safest.

So what was he doing?

He flipped open his mobile laptop and connected to the secure Wi-Fi in his car. He needed to read the research on Lincoln Brown. Because that was where it all started.

Lincoln Brown was currently an upstanding member of the community. Yet there were a few hints, not on the public record, that perhaps he had not been squeaky clean.

He had started as a janitor at a museum in his late teens then moved on to a security guard. He'd apparently listened while all those docents were talking about art. He'd begun to paint and apprenticed with the recently deceased Jonathon Harrington the Third, a moderately famous painter and famous art restorer, who recognized Brown's love of art even without a formal education. Brown subsequently became a very sought-after art restorer and appraiser.

His wife of fifty-odd years had died last year after a long battle with cancer.

He currently resided in a very fancy part of DC, however the house was in his daughter-in-law's name. He had a decent stock portfolio but most of his investments appeared to be in art.

He and his deceased wife had one son, Ayesha's father, who married an extremely old-money-wealthy white woman and currently lived in Europe.

One grandchild, Ayesha.

Marsh needed to figure out why Lincoln was worried about his granddaughter. He thought back to that meeting. She knew what her grandfather was referring to. She didn't outright say she didn't need a bodyguard. She said she didn't want one. Something really didn't add up. Which was why he was here.

Marsh stared up at the windows on the fourth floor of the renovated industrial building. It was two in the morning and her lights were still on. He wondered what she was doing.

Earlier in the day, he'd also requested an intensive background check on Ayesha Brown hoping he wouldn't need to violate her privacy. But after reading the info on Lincoln Brown, he concluded that he was going to have to read the report Kita had just sent. *Thank you, Kita.*

Maybe he should have just let this go. But Jill and Kita had both urged him to investigate a little further if for no other reason than to make sure his father wasn't steering them into another clusterfuck.

Preliminary results showed that Ayesha Brown owned the loft outright. Had no car. Had a small amount of credit card debt. She had attended art school at the very prestigious Beaux Arts in Paris and lived with her grandparents before and after she attended college. Her parents had transferred guardianship of their daughter to her grandparents when she was thirteen.

That was a little odd.

He dug further into the report. Kita had included more personal information. Ayesha had had three serious relationships. But no one right now. And he hated that he was happy about that.

He couldn't get that moment in the hallway out of his mind. Electricity had arced between them, and the temptation to see if her lips were as soft as they looked had been hard to ignore. Although, if she was talking, she was pissing him off.

Letting go of her details, he studied the area. The neighborhood was sketch. Litter in doorways and signs of the homeless juxtaposed against a charming little flower shop with a striped awning and French lettering on the windows, an old-fashioned barbershop complete with the red, blue, and white pole, and a Korean takeout restaurant. Ayesha Brown's building was a converted factory with large windowed areas, brick siding, and a corrugated tin roof. A giant freight elevator that appeared to be solely for freight was next to one regular door which seemed to be the entrance. And it didn't look secure or safe.

Based on the research he'd done on her family, she could likely afford an apartment in a more upscale neighborhood. So what she was doing here?

He took a sip of cold coffee and seriously questioned his sanity. She had intrigued him. He rubbed a hand over his tired face and glanced at the report on her again. There was nothing in her background that raised red flags. Sure, her grandfather had some areas of concern, but they were old. Over fifteen years. Nothing that would relate to her, she had been an early teenager the last time there was anything remotely questionable.

This was a waste of time. And yet he couldn't bring himself to leave.

An hour later, he was just about to go home to his lonely sterile condo when a slight figure walked confidently down the sidewalk. They looked both ways and Marsh slumped down in his driver's seat, watching curiously. A hoodie concealed the person's face and gender. They crossed the street with a skip in their step and he would have ignored them, except they stopped at the entrance to Ayesha's building. They slipped something from their pocket and seconds later the door to her building opened. He would have assumed it was another tenant. Except for the furtive little glance before they crept inside the building.

Marsh's hackles raised. Something about that person was off.

What were the odds that they were up to no good? One hundred percent. He sat in the car for five seconds, arguing with his conscience. Could be nothing. Just because they seemed furtive didn't mean they were going after Ayesha. But that little flicker of fear in her eyes before she'd turned his assistance down flat kept prodding at his subconscious.

Fuck it.

He slipped from his car and closed the door with a soft thunk. Nearly mimicking the figure, he glanced both ways, then crossed the street. When he got to the entrance to her building, his suspicions were confirmed. Whoever had just entered had broken the locks. They'd taken a small tool to the doorjamb, splintering the wood around the brass fittings. The person had clearly jammed something, a metal pin or file, in one of them, and the door wasn't shut all the way.

That was not the action of a tenant. Especially in this neighborhood.

Ayesha was on the fourth floor. Marsh crept up the industrial stairs, taking care not to make any noise.

He kept hearing "She needs a bodyguard" in his father's voice echoing in his brain. Marsh moved with a stealthy speed. He would just confirm that no one was trying to get into her loft and then he'd leave. Abandon this crazy need to check in on her and go home and get some sleep.

He rounded the platform on the second-floor landing and didn't see anyone in the hallway, just as he heard Ayesha shout, "Hey!"

UGH. She needed to go to bed. It was 3:30 in the morning and she hadn't made any progress on the crowning piece for her show. The four-by-six-foot canvas rested against the far wall untouched. Instead she'd been playing with lines and color on a slightly smaller canvas since she got home. The oil and mixed media bore a striking resemblance to the object of her ire. Ever since she had left Uncle Bobby's office, she couldn't get that douchebag out of her head.

But she wasn't remembering his asshole-ness, she was remembering the slice of his cheekbone, the curve of his mouth, the breadth of his shoulders, and the inquisitive intelligence in his gaze.

No matter what her brain thought of Marsh Adams, her body thought he was hot.

Her whole body ached. It had been a long day. Full of surprises and mental anguish. She was pretty sure she knew what she had to do, but she had absolutely no idea how she was going to do it.

In the shadowed darkness, she cleaned her brushes at the utility sink she'd had installed in the corner. Her painting area was set up to take advantage of the natural light coming in from the windows. Of course there was no light now since it was half past way beyond her bedtime. Once she was done cleaning the brushes, the comforting scent of linseed oil lingered in her nose. She used soap and water to clean the oil and paint off her hands. She thought she heard a noise over the drumming of water in the deep plastic basin.

It was late. No one else in the building should be out and about. Even her party girl neighbor was already home and in bed.

She shut off the water and grabbed for the towel on the rack to the right of the sink. It was probably nothing. She turned around. Because *nothing* had just cast a shadow on her wall.

"Hey!" she shouted. Her heart boomed against her ribcage. She needed a weapon and fast. But shit, her pepper spray was safely stowed in her hobo bag by the front door.

The figure in the doorway said nothing. At first she thought the hoodie was obscuring his or her face. But then she realized they were wearing a mask and gloves. She was too far from the kitchen and any kind of weapon. Ayesha reached behind her and grabbed for the mason jar where her brushes were soaking in the linseed oil. The oil muddled with paint was her only option.

"What the hell do you want?" Ayesha kept the jar behind her back.

They said nothing, advancing slowly as if they had all the time in the world.

"You need to leave." The quaver in her voice pissed her

off. Who the hell was this person to come into her home and scare her?

The figure was still silent as they stalked toward her. "Get. Out."

But the man—why she thought it was a man she didn't know, something in the way he moved—just shook his head.

Ayesha edged toward the door but at some point she'd have to pass him. She didn't want to leave this asshole in her condo with her paintings. They were her life.

"What do you want? Who sent you?" She shot questions at them.

They just shook their head again and continued to advance.

Ayesha made a dash for the door, gripping the glass jar with the linseed oil in her right hand. Paintings weren't as important as her life.

He grabbed her left arm, and she swung around and tossed the jar at his face. The oil hit him in the face, and the glass crashed to the floor, breaking on the sealed cement. He let go of her with an unearthly scream. Peripherally she noted the thunder of footsteps in her hallway.

The intruder released her with a snarl and ran for the door.

Marsh Adams burst into her apartment. *What was he doing here?* "Are you okay?"

The intruder barreled into Marsh and knocked him into the wall.

"Y-yeah, yes," Ayesha stuttered. She didn't want the guy to get away. She leapt toward the door, forgetting about being barefoot and the broken glass. "Ouch, dammit!"

She saw the moment Marsh chose not to go after the intruder. He rushed over to her.

"What are you doing?" she cried. "He's getting away!"

"Are you okay?"

The pain in her foot, which had been numbed flared to life. Ow. "He's getting away!"

"Your safety is more important."

"What are you talking about?"

"You don't know if they had a partner." Marsh's gaze raked over her. "What did you do to them?"

"Threw linseed oil and paint at him."

"Smart thinking." Marsh smiled and she wanted to preen at the admiration in his gaze. "Him?"

"I think so." Something about the build, he was slender, as if maybe he wasn't a full-grown adult. "But young, maybe. White skin showed in the holes for the eyes and mouth, but I couldn't tell what color eyes."

"Anything else?"

"He didn't speak. Not a word."

"If I was going to attack someone, this would be the perfect time," Marsh said. "He wasn't expecting you to be awake. He expected you to be in bed. Asleep."

Ayesha shivered, thinking about what could have happened. She was glad that she'd been awake, obsessing about the man standing in front of her now.

"This wasn't random. He broke into your building and headed right to your apartment." Marsh glanced around. "If he'd been surveilling the building, he would have noticed that your light was still on. Instead he went right for you."

The terror that had frozen her brain was wearing off. And a lot of other things started to register. Such as... "What are you doing here?"

"Well, I was planning on rushing in to save the day, but you took care of it all on your own." There was approval in his voice and...wonder?

She had. Even if she had been flat-out terrified. "My Gramps always said to use what you've got."

"He's an interesting guy."

She didn't think he meant it as a compliment. But before she could snark back at him, he glanced down.

A small puddle of blood pooled on the floor.

"Shit. Hold on." He lifted her in his arms as if she were a twig.

"What are you doing?"

He ignored her and strode over to the counter where she kept her supplies. He set her on the utilitarian Formica gently and lifted her foot. He winced. "Clean towels anywhere?"

"Drawer to your right." He retrieved a hand towel and dampened it with water and proceeded to clean out the cut on the bottom of her foot. If you had asked her this morning if Marsh Adams had a nurturing bone in his body, she would have said, "Not a chance."

Instead he carefully extracted the chunk of glass she'd stepped on with a gentleness that was unexpected.

"Band-Aids?"

Yes. She had a lot of Band-Aids. She tended to cut her hands and skin when she was working with other media.

"Bathroom," she said huskily. "Top drawer on the left."

"Be right back." He brushed his thumb over her cheekbone in a subtle caress. And then he was gone.

Back again a minute later, he carefully coated the cut with Neosporin and pressed a Band-Aid over it. His thumb mimicked the caress on her face, stroking over the arch in her foot in a seductive rhythm. Her eyes were glued to that mesmerizing caress.

Heat rose between them, fierce and intense. He cradled

her foot in his big palms, the calluses on his fingers indicating that he didn't just sit at a desk.

Her lady bits responded to the fairly innocuous touch as if he had stripped her naked and put his hands all over her. Electricity arced, zapping her clit. Tingles spread throughout her body in a wave of desire. Praise Jesus, this man pushed all her buttons.

Then she dropped her gaze. Marsh Adams had a gun—a gun!—in a holster on his right hip.

"You have a gun?"

He smirked. "Typically bodyguards do."

Well, that put her back up. "I said I didn't want one."

"How's that working out for you?"

Fuck. He had a point.

$$\text{———————————————}$$

Chapter 5

$$\text{———————————————}$$

He wanted to kiss her.

So badly that if she spread her legs just a little wider, he was going to step into that void, cup her mule-ish jaw in his hand, and take her mouth with his.

The pupils in her mesmerizing hazel eyes dilated. She inhaled a quick little breath, lifting her collarbones. Her large shirt, splattered with more paint, dipped off one shoulder. One bare shoulder, revealing that she was, once again, braless.

Without his command, his gaze dipped to her breasts. Her nipples were hard points against the cotton, and his hands literally tingled with the need to touch her.

Desire swirled between them in a vortex of adrenaline and mistrust. Marsh forced his hands into fists so that he didn't commit an inappropriate act. Her pulse thudded in the hollow of her throat as he catalogued her body's physiological responses.

But the reality was the response could also be an adrenaline letdown.

And he wasn't about to take advantage of her fear.

"Stay there while I clean up the glass."

"I can clean up my own glass." She put her hands on the edge of the countertop and readied to jump down.

He knew how to get her to stay. "Well, that's just stupid. I have on shoes and you don't."

As expected, calling her stupid didn't go over well. She put her hands on her hips in a saucy move and cocked her head at him. "I can clean up my own mess."

"Let me take care of this, please."

"Fine." She collapsed back against the wall and hunched her shoulders. "What does bodyguarding have to do with public relations?"

Marsh didn't even pause as he swept the glass into a small pile. "I used to be a US Marshal."

"That's not an answer."

"I have experience protecting witnesses, clients." He focused on the task, hoping she'd answer honestly. "What do you think he wanted?"

Marsh pushed the glass into the dustpan, his heart clenching at the blood on the floor. He wasn't squeamish, so why those small drops of blood bothered him, he couldn't articulate.

"Just a random mugging."

"Not a chance." Marsh dumped the glass into a paper bag.

"What are you doing?"

"I'll have a lab analyze the blood and see if you cut him."

"A lab." She eyed him suspiciously. "Again, that doesn't sound much like public relations."

"I have a friend who owes me a favor."

"Aren't you special? You have a friend." She shook her

head, her Afro bouncing against her cheeks. "I don't need your help."

"Are you seriously telling me that after this break-in, you don't want a bodyguard?"

"In case you haven't noticed, this is a changing neighborhood. I just need to get better locks."

Marsh snorted. "Yeah, that's what you needed, better locks." There was no way she could miss the sarcasm in his voice. Jesus, she rubbed him the wrong way. Except for when he wanted to rub her the right way.

"I'm sure it was nothing." She appeared to have brushed off her fear and adrenaline and was back to the spirited woman from earlier. "So…you were stalking me?"

Marsh sighed. "Of course not."

"Well, you can go on home now. I'm fine."

Something about that easy dismissal rankled him. She had been scared. No question about it. And while she had fought off the intruder, the outcome might have been different if Marsh hadn't shown up. He wanted to shake her and get her to take this situation more seriously. And he didn't even know what the situation was.

He stepped closer to where she sat on the counter. "So you're just going to, what? Go back to painting and pretend this didn't happen?"

She jerked her chin up. "Pretty much."

"Just forget that he was here. That *I* was here."

"Yep."

He couldn't even explain why that thought jerked his chain but her casual dismissal chafed. She needed some common sense. She needed a serious dose of fear and caution.

And no way was he going to let her forget that he was here. He stepped between her parted thighs and her breath caught. She inhaled quickly, those hard points taunting him. Marsh cupped her face in his left hand and held her still, his grip on her bare shoulder with his right. His thumb stroked up and down the long elegant line of her neck. "I'm going to kiss you."

"I don't think so." She put her hands on him for the first time. Her fingers curled through the belt loops of his jeans, and she yanked him toward her. He thudded up against the V in her legs, and she slid her hands up his chest and tugged his head toward her. "I'm going to kiss you."

SHE HAD MEANT the move as a distraction. A way to make him forget what he was asking about. But the moment her lips touched his, everything changed.

His mouth was softer than she'd anticipated. She had drawn the curve of his lips and the shape of his jaw and the cut of his cheekbones over and over again but hadn't been able to get them quite right.

She gave herself permission to touch him. To learn the curves and the textures of his body. Stubble abraded her palms as she spread her fingers over his face, tracing each angle and curve as if there would be a test on it later.

At first he held back, even though he had been the one to instigate the contact. His body was stiff and unmoving, even as his mouth devoured hers. Ayesha pulled back slightly, scraping her nails along the base of his neck and into his thick unruly hair. She nipped at his chin, then licked the spot.

With a groan he gave in to their mutual desire. He stepped closer until his erection, hot and hard behind the zipper of his jeans, pushed against her leggings-clad sex.

As he requested entrance with his tongue, his hands skimmed over her shoulders and down her arms. He laced his fingers with hers and lifted her hands above her head stretching her body out for him like a banquet. She arched into his hard chest, rubbing her nipples against his muscles. Now she was the one groaning as he stroked his erection against her. She wanted her hands free to explore his body. To learn each mountain and valley and commit them to memory so that the next time she couldn't sleep for thinking about him, she would be able to commit him to canvas.

He kept her hands pinned above her head in one of his while his other hand skimmed over her collarbones and then slid down her body to cup her breast. She panted when he came up for air. He pinched her nipple lightly, causing another moan.

He kissed his way along her jaw and nipped at her earlobe.

"Let my hands go," she demanded. Her voice was husky, aroused.

She needed to touch him. The ache was nearly physical.

He stilled completely. Dropped her hands. And stepped so quickly away from her as if she had a toxic disease, and he didn't want to catch it.

"We can't do this." He turned around and surveyed her loft. "I'll wait with you until the cops get here."

"Cops?"

"Yeah."

She had no intention of calling the cops. Harrington the Fourth had been explicitly clear in his threats. Call law enforcement and he would send them whatever dirt he had regarding her grandfather's past indiscretions. She had no way of knowing if this break-in was related, although, come on, how could it not be? But she refused to do anything that might jeopardize her grandfather. "There's no need for you to wait."

He spun back around and eyed her. Suspiciously. "You aren't going to call the cops, are you?"

Again, the only thing to do was go on the offensive. "You're right. Someone like me calls the cops, I'm just as likely to get arrested."

"What are you talking about?"

"Look at the color of my skin. I call this in and I'm just as likely to be the one being questioned extensively." She hopped down from the counter. "No, thank you."

"As much as I wish you were wrong, I agree. But I would be with you."

She had a deep distrust of law enforcement even without this current threat. But it definitely meant she couldn't ignore the problem like her Gramps wanted to do.

Apparently Harrington wasn't bluffing. She was going to have to take matters into her own hands. He had upped the stakes by coming after her.

The only way to make this right was to steal the original paintings back from Harrington and get the fakes from his father's estate and switch them.

So, in addition to her show, she was going to have to figure out how to become a thief.

Marsh Adams wasn't letting go of his questioning. "Who threatened you?"

"I have no idea." But with the way he looked at her, she could tell he knew she was lying. Tough. "It's time for you to go, Mr. Adams."

"You're sure you feel comfortable here alone?"

Of course she wasn't. But he didn't make her feel any more comfortable. And if he stayed, she'd be tempted to do something really ill-advised like jump his bones. And she couldn't afford to cozy up to a former US Marshal who ran a "PR" business and had lab people who owed him favors.

"I can stand guard," he offered.

"Not necessary. I've been taking care of myself for a long time." She shooed him out the door. After all, she had a heist to plan.

Chapter 6

Marsh settled into the front seat of his car. He would have to wait until labs opened to take the bag of glass to be analyzed. In the meantime, he could get to work on finding whoever broke into her loft.

Marsh sighed and pulled out his phone.

He called the first hospital on his list and gave a law enforcement alias that the company used for pretexting. "I'm wondering if you've had anyone check into the emergency room with possible vision damage from chemicals. White male or female, slight build."

After calling the nearest five hospital emergency rooms, he acknowledged defeat. Using a pretext wasn't going to work. The technique skated a gray area as it was. And apparently the hospitals knew their rights and refused to release any information. But two hospitals had hesitated. There was no help for it. He needed to call Kita.

He dialed her number and waited impatiently.

"This had better be good," his old pal muttered huskily. The rumble of a male voice in the background surprised him. US Marshal Alex Saunders. While Marsh had been off trying to right his wrongs and correct the massive mistake that he'd made in believing their client, Kita had gone and gotten herself a boyfriend. She seemed happy. And Saunders seemed like a pretty good guy. But it still surprised him that his old friend had let down her guard so quickly.

"Can you hack into these two hospitals and see if they've done patient intake on a white male or female with an eye injury in the last hour."

"Everything okay?" The sleep was gone from her voice and she was all business.

"Someone attacked Ayesha Brown in her loft."

"And how would you know that?"

"I was staking out her residence."

Kita laughed softly. "Stalker much?"

"It paid off, didn't it?"

"Give me a second."

He heard the rustle of her covers and the clacking of her fingers on the keyboard as she worked her cyber magic.

"Okay. Give me everything you've got."

Marsh relayed the details that he knew.

"How did you hurt them?"

"It wasn't me. Ayesha threw a glass and potentially burned their eyes with chemicals."

"Sounds as if I'd like this girl."

"You probably would."

"So you couldn't rush in and save the day?"

No, he couldn't. It was weird how much that disturbed him. And yet he loved that Ayesha had saved herself. "She didn't need me at all."

"You rushed into her apartment to save her…while she was kicking ass."

"Pretty much."

"Why didn't the cops look into this?"

"She wouldn't call them."

Kita was silent. Then she said, "That's not a good sign, Marsh."

"I am aware."

"Especially coming on the heels of the request for a bodyguard."

"I would agree." Marsh's gaze bounced around the interior of his Mercedes, touching on the burled wood and the black leather seats. He had offered his help, twice, and she had turned him down flat. She didn't want the police called.

"She's definitely hiding something," Marsh said.

"Maybe you need to back away from this, from her," Kita said softly. "Let her handle it."

He knew he should. She could clearly take care of herself. She was clearly lying. But for some reason he couldn't seem to back off.

"While you're at it, set up a tracker on the GPS signal on her phone." See, he wasn't taking her at face value. "That way we can keep tabs on her."

"Didn't you just promise Jill that you were going to do everything in your power to make up for the clusterfuck that was Brianna Walsh?"

He had.

"Let it go, Marsh."

But he couldn't.

MARSH DRAGGED himself into work later that morning.

He parked in the back lot and headed inside through the rear vestibule. The new wood where the repairs had been made after someone had attempted to break in a few weeks ago stood out like a sore thumb. He quickly went through the several layers of security measures—biometric readings, alpha-numeric passwords, and visual checkpoints—before he gained entrance to their building. He waved to Viktor, who should be in the booth today, and then headed toward his office.

He grabbed his cup of coffee at the credenza in their conference room and snatched a cookie from the tray of jolly brown-faced Santa cookies decorated with sparkling red frosting and white crystals for the suit.

Yes! Maria Torres had been baking again. After a particularly fascinating discussion during a company meeting, he had learned that growing up in her Latinx household, Santa had brown skin. Totally made sense but still surprised him. And her cookies were the bomb. He took a bite of the decadent treat and headed upstairs with his mug of coffee, determined to get a jump on the day, even if he did feel like ass.

Jill came barreling out of her office. "We have a problem."

"What's wrong?"

She gripped the *Washington Post* in her fist. "ALIAS has been in the news too much lately. Some intrepid reporter decided to go digging."

She waved the paper; its headline questioned ALIAS's PR status and insinuated that they were engaged in illegal activity.

"It's all bullshit of course." Jill rubbed her temples. "But we don't need the exposure."

This was his fault. They could have weathered the other small inconsistencies. But the situation with Brianna Walsh and the fallout from getting that fixed had brought their company to the attention of too many federal agencies.

They had known this was a possibility after Marsh's screwup last month. But he'd naïvely begun to hope that it wasn't going to be a problem.

"Let's game out scenarios on what to do."

Jill pressed a key on her laptop, and the printer in the corner began to spit out paper. "We have a couple of options."

"We can just continue to deny everything and say our clients are private." But Marsh knew that was a desperate wish. Back when they had operated under the radar, that explanation would work. But because of his actions over the last few months, there were questions from multiple agencies. And they had had inquiries from several people regarding some of their clients. Their reputation and their business were built on a model of complete secrecy. They even had a small public relations branch, but in a completely different building across town. And they did very little PR work.

Jill propped both her elbows on her desk and put her head in her hands, rubbing her temples. "We need some serious damage control."

"What options have you come up with?"

"One. We should consider actually doing some PR work."

That hadn't really come up as one of the possibilities that he had entertained. Marsh verbalized the idea that had been rumbling around in his brain since his meeting with his father. "Another possibility is to actually take some clients who just need basic protection."

Jillian cocked her head as if contemplating the idea. "Let ourselves be seen working a different kind of case?"

"Just one or two. Or maybe we even give the reporter something."

The more they denied, the more likely it was that the reporters would keep digging.

She grimaced. "I hate having to deal with reporters. And I hate that our clients might be in jeopardy."

She left unspoken the fact that she hated that this was all his fault.

"How do I fix this?" Marsh just needed to know what to do. How to make his relationship with Jillian go back to normal.

"Time," Jill said. "The only way to heal this trust breach is time."

"Fine. I have plenty of that." And that was true. He planned to do everything within his power to make up his actions to his partner. He remembered Ayesha's initial interest when she thought he might give her PR help. "So then maybe we just need to give them one of our clients."

"What the hell do you mean by that?" Jill jammed her fists on her hips.

"PR client."

"Oh." Jill deflated. She tapped her finger on the headline that clever brain of hers running at warp speed. "That's actually not a bad idea."

An idea was taking shape in his brain. Ayesha Brown wouldn't accept a bodyguard. But she might accept public relations help.

They went into her office so that Marsh could explain the past twelve hours. "I promise that I won't do anything to jeopardize the company."

But they both knew it was already too late. This article wasn't going to be an easy fix. Because now that the questions had started, journalists were going to be probing Adams-Larsen looking for inconsistencies.

"Okay. What are you thinking?"

"We let it leak that we're doing PR for Ayesha Brown's show." If Marsh could convince Ayesha to accept an Adams-Larsen public relations campaign for her upcoming show, then he could spend time with her and maybe also solve the mystery of who wanted to hurt her family.

"It's a little suspicious that after years of extreme privacy, suddenly we name our clients," Jill said.

"We give an interview. And we say that we're changing our model and if clients are willing to be identified, then we will let that happen," Marsh replied.

"It's not a bad idea. It could work." Jill shrugged. "Honestly, I've been thinking that perhaps it's time for us to be more public about our services. And diversify."

The reason they had begun in secrecy was to protect their clients. The level of encryption and layers of secrecy regarding the relocations of their clients had never been broken. They segmented their employee duties so that no one person knew everything about a relocation. Brianna had been an exception because Marsh had inserted himself into the entire process. As long as they stuck to the protocols they had put in place, their clients would be safe.

"I'm pretty sure I can convince Ayesha Brown to take the PR help."

"We'll need to meet with Zara."

Zara Cooper, their PR manager, worked in another building far away from the secretive nature of their witness protection and relocation business.

"Let's have her work up a promotion plan and explain it to us." Jill was already making notes at her desk.

Marsh was thinking about logistics. He needed to approach Ayesha with the plan as soon as possible. "Let's send Jake to pick Zara up."

"That works." Jill pressed a button on the intercom and requested his presence in her office.

Marsh asked. "Has he been a little moody lately?"

"The whole office has been moody lately."

Which was likely due to his screwups. "Okay. Let's get her here and iron out a plan for Ayesha. I need to have a concrete plan in place in order to convince her that she needs our services." It needed to be kick-ass.

Jill hesitated. "I'm working another angle as well."

Another angle? "You want to share?"

"Not yet." She glanced at her watch. "As a matter of fact, I've got a meeting in a few minutes."

"I'll let you get to it." Marsh yawned.

"You look like shit."

"Spent the night in my car." He yawned again and wished he had time for a shower.

"There should be easier ways to get someone to accept help. Maybe you just need to cut her loose," she said reluctantly. "We can come up with another PR client."

But he couldn't. Although he didn't think convincing Ayesha would be easy.

In fact, Marsh wouldn't be surprised if she turned them down. He would just have to change her mind.

THERE WERE PROBABLY BETTER ways to go about this and he was tired, but he didn't care.

He glanced around the neighborhood, taking in the bars on the windows, the broken glass on the street, and the needles in the alley next to her building. She was an adult, clearly. She could live where she wanted, but his stomach couldn't help but clench at the signs the neighborhood was far from safe.

He leaned on the bell and listened for a buzzer but none came. He pressed on the intercom button again. Nothing.

No help for it. He sighed and took out his cell. With a deep shrug he dialed his father.

"Marsh," his father said heartily. "Good to hear from you, son."

"Yeah, can I get Ayesha Brown's phone number?"

There was a heavy pause on the other side of the line. "Why do you want her phone number?"

"Because I'm going to try to convince her to…work with me." He kept it vague. It was none of the judge's business.

"Well, in that case…."

Anger started to burn beneath his breastbone. "So what, if I'd been asking for personal reasons, you wouldn't have given it to me?"

"Of course I would've given it to you." The judge hesitated. "But I'd also tell you that her grandfather means a lot to your mother and me, and Ayesha is like a niece to me."

"You didn't try and bang her?" Marsh blurted the words out of the shame burning through him.

"There's no call for that kind of language, Marsh."

Marsh couldn't help it, it seemed as if whenever he got inside his father's sphere of influence, he was compelled to be nasty.

The judge said tiredly, "I'm sorry."

What the what? The judge had just apologized…to him? "For what?"

"I'm sorry I let you down. All those years ago."

"How about you be sorry for hurting mom?" Marsh's jaw was tight. "She's the one who matters."

"Marsh…." His father was uncharacteristically at a loss for words. "I'm sorry I hurt *you*."

He didn't want to feel for the old man, but he'd sounded tired. Old. Defeated.

"It doesn't matter." They both knew that was a lie.

"Here is Ayesha's cell." The judge rattled off a ten-digit phone number and then said, "Good luck."

Yeah, Marsh figured he was going to need it. He quickly dialed Ayesha's phone number and waited.

The call went straight to voicemail. She couldn't know it was him unless she had super-secret hacking skills that he was unaware of, so she wasn't avoiding *him* per se. She was just avoiding people.

He needed to talk to her. It was late morning so hopefully she'd gotten some sleep. God knows he hadn't. He could just go in. The lock was still broken. But Marsh didn't want to betray her trust.

He rang the bell again. But nothing happened. In complete exasperation he rang the bell for 4A, her next-door neighbor.

"Can I help you?"

"Trying to get a hold of Ayesha. Is she home?"

"I'm sure if she wanted you to know, she would let you know." Sassy.

"I just wanted to check in with her after the break-in last night."

"Break-in! Get up here." Now that he had permission to enter the building, Marsh opened the door quickly before Ayesha's neighbor changed her mind. He walked up the stairs slowly. When he got to the fourth floor, the neighbor was standing in her doorway with the door open. The young white woman with blue eyes and long straight blonde hair wore a tight black spandex camisole and loose sweats that hung low on her hips. She had smudges of mascara under her eyes as if she'd just woken up. "Is everything okay?"

"She scared him off, but I wanted to check on her."

Now the neighbor narrowed her gaze. "She scared him off?"

"Yeah. I got here a little late." It was amazing how much that truth burned. He was used to doing the saving.

"How come I haven't seen you around before?"

"We just met." All technically true but he'd bet that Ayesha wouldn't classify their relationship that way.

"Oh, well, nice to meet you. I'm Bethany." She stuck out her hand and Marsh shook it carefully and then dropped it quickly.

"Thanks for letting me in."

"Sure thing. Although I hear music. Which means you may not want to interrupt her. Am I right?" She laughed a little trill of enjoyment and then shut her door.

Marsh strode over to 4B and knocked on the door carefully. Bethany was correct. The music was blaring some bluesy, jazzy mix with soulful horns and a flute. For a few minutes he didn't think she was going to answer. But finally she yanked the door open and barked, "What?"

Ayesha blinked at Marsh as if she'd never seen him before, her gaze blurry and unfocused. She frowned, clearly trying to connect the dots. She wasn't expecting him.

"Can I come in?"

"Seriously?" She propped her hands on her hips. The button-up shirt she wore hung on her frame, splattered with paint again, more paint in her hair and a spot right next to her nose where she clearly had an itch. She didn't have any makeup on, and her skin was clear and beautiful. She blinked at him, her lashes thick against her cheekbones.

"I'd like to talk," he said again patiently when she still hadn't quite acknowledged his presence.

"Now really isn't a good time." She started to close the door in his face.

But Marsh stuck his foot in to stop her. "I have a proposition for you."

She snorted. "I'll bet you do." She gave him a saucy look and skimmed her gaze over his body. He had changed clothes from last night, another pair of jeans and a light sweater. What he wore when he didn't have client meetings. Loafers. A rough worn leather jacket that had seen better days.

"Not that kind."

She looked at him for another second and then said, "Pity."

His heart beat harder at the insinuation. Because it was a pity. But that wasn't why he was here. And that was strictly off the table. "Sorry that can't happen again."

"Fine. Come on in." She strode over to a glass jar near the sink and dropped the brush she was holding into the liquid—whatever she had burned the guy with last night.

"Have a seat." She gestured carefully at the modern white leather sofa in the far corner of the loft. It rested atop a very shaggy rug with long strands of cream and white and was flanked by an end table in spare modern lines on one side and an Eames chair in white with a footrest on the other. She wore ratty paint-splattered clothes but had an Eames chair and sofa in her living room. Ayesha Brown was a study in contrasts and Marsh would love to study her longer.

He shook himself out of the sexual stupor she'd managed to induce, sat carefully on the expensive sofa, and waited until she took the chair. She plopped her feet up on the footrest one over the other, her bare toes painted in a rainbow of polish. Marsh stared at those bare feet, wanting to run his finger over her delicate arch and make her shiver like she had last night. The bandage was a stark reminder of the kiss that happened after he'd tended to her foot.

Focus on the problem at hand. This was all about getting ALIAS cover for their other business. "I was thinking about what the judge said yesterday, and I would like to offer you our public relations services."

"*You* do public relations?"

"Actually, you'd be working with a team of us. But I would be the point person."

"That won't work for me."

He'd thought after yesterday in the judge's office that she would at the very least consider it before she turned him down. In reality she should be jumping at the chance. "Is another agency handling the promotion?"

"You really have experience doing promo for an art show?" Ayesha raised an eyebrow. "Great. Show me your portfolio."

He was at a loss. He was usually much smarter with women, but for some reason she threw him totally off. "You're clearly in the middle of work," he said. "Maybe we should discuss this over dinner."

That would give him time to refine his approach.

"Not necessary." She eyed him suspiciously "How much is it going to cost?"

"I feel like we can work that out." Marsh smiled his "you can trust me, I used to be a Marshal" smile. Nothing.

"Again, how much?"

"It would be pro bono because you're a friend of the judge's."

"Your super-wonderful daddy. Oh, who you can't

stand." She propped her hands on her hips again and those hard points of her nipples taunted him. Did she ever wear a bra?

"My relationship with him is…complicated." That was the understatement of the decade. "But I'd really like to help you."

AYESHA STUDIED MARSH ADAMS. Something else was going on here, but she'd come to the realization at five this morning—when she was still awake and extremely jittery from adrenaline—that she couldn't get ready for her show and figure out how she was going to steal those paintings back and keep an eye on her own safety.

She had already concluded that she needed to reach out to Marsh Adams and see if he might be interested in the bodyguard position. Even if she really, really didn't want one.

Her Gramps trusted the judge and that was enough for her. But now, she was questioning what was really going on. Why was Marsh Adams suddenly offering her PR work? She'd done a little digging when she couldn't sleep, and there was an article in today's paper about his company and some strange goings-on. It made it seem like they were not really a PR firm.

On the other hand, she couldn't afford to say no at this point. Because the reality was if she couldn't steal those paintings back, they were going to need money for her Gramps's lawyer and defense against Harrington. And with that realization her knee jerk reaction to his offer of PR and mini rebellion was at an end. Ugh. "Okay."

His eyebrows rose. His dirty blond hair flopped over one

eye. His eyebrows were darker than his hair, a light brown that he quirked as he smiled as if he couldn't help it.

"Okay…?"

"Okay, thank you for the PR help," she said grudgingly. See, she could be polite.

"And dinner?"

"I'm in the middle of this." *This* being nothing because she couldn't concentrate and kept drawing pictures of the man across from her. But she needed time to get her armor on and get her battle plan in place. And she needed time to figure out exactly what he was actually up to. Which she couldn't do on two hours' sleep.

"I'll meet you—"

"I'll pick you up," he said at the exact same time.

It wasn't a date. However, she didn't have a car. "Fine. You can pick me up. But let's make it an early dinner."

"Sounds good." He named a time, then stood. "I'll see you in a few hours."

He left quickly. She stared at her steel door and wondered…*what have I done?*

Chapter 7

Marsh took the afternoon off to go see his mother.

Yes, he'd been dreading it. His mother…and his father? He literally couldn't stomach the thought. He walked up the wide porch steps to his childhood home.

Miniature topiaries in stone pots stood sentinel at the base of the steps. Evergreen garland wrapped in white lights draped the railings, tied at intervals with big red puffy bows. The doorway was flanked with more urns filled with birch branches of varying heights, decorated with little white lights and more red bows. His mother could give Martha Stewart a run for her money.

Every year the decorations were different but always festive. And he'd be lying if he said that he didn't like them. Elaborate decorations for every season were an integral part of his childhood. His mother brought magic to the holiday season. And he loved her for it. Because even when her heart was hurting, she made the world a more beautiful place.

Marsh knocked on the front door and then used his key to go inside.

Toeing off his shoes, he left them by the mat. Three-foot-tall nutcrackers guarded the living room. A large evergreen that topped seven feet and smelled of Christmas and holidays past sat in the front picture window. Multicolored lights were wrapped around the tree, and glass Christmas balls of all shapes and sizes glittered, reflecting the lights back at him. An angel perched atop the tree, the glow of her halo bright in the darkened room.

"Mom?" Marsh walked toward the kitchen. "I'm home."

For a moment, there was nothing, and then his mother burst from the kitchen.

She was baking Christmas cookies—sugar cookies, pecan snowballs, and almond rings. Almond and pecan, sugar and rum scented the air. A German ancestor from way back had passed down the recipes from generation to generation. They were holiday staples at his house, and the smells brought back a rush of memories of Christmases past.

"Marsh!" His mother rushed into the living room, an apron around her still trim middle and a smudge of green sugar sparkled on her left cheekbone. She enveloped him in a hug, her arms wrapping around him and squeezing. Marsh's throat tightened and he returned the hug. He had missed his mother.

While he had been gone tracking down a criminal, he had kept in touch with his mother, talking to her on the phone every few weeks. But talking on the phone was no substitute for an in-person hug.

"Why didn't you tell me you were coming? I would've made lunch."

"I can't stay long. I've got a dinner thing."

"A date?" She smiled with a twinkle in her eye, only half teasing him.

"Work."

"Honey, you need to make sure you have some balance in your life."

"I'll get some balance next year. Right now I've got to make up for some things."

"Is everything okay?" She pressed her palm against his biceps and squeezed.

"It will be." He was going to make sure of it. But currently he had to bring up something that he was dreading.

His mother's smile faded and her eyebrows crinkled.

"We need to talk."

She sighed. "Been waiting for this conversation." She pivoted around on her toes and headed back into the kitchen. "This calls for a cookie or ten."

There wasn't much that couldn't be solved by his mother's cookies, but he had a feeling this might be one of those times.

His mother pulled out one of the oak chairs that had graced this room since he was a kid, and sat at the old, scarred farm table. "Let's get this over with."

Since she knew what he was talking about, he dove right in. "You…." Turns out he couldn't say it. "And dad?"

His mother flushed, her face getting red in the warm kitchen air. And he didn't think it was from the heat of the stove. Dammit, he really didn't want to have this conversation, but what the hell was she thinking?

"It's complicated."

His father, the cheating bastard, had destroyed his mother. "He hurt you."

"We never talked about this because I knew it would upset you." Mom blinked and looked away.

"I'm not a child, Mom."

"You are a man. One I'm extremely proud of."

"I just…don't understand." Marsh pressed his palms flat on the table, remembering the morning she'd put her head on this very slab and cried her eyes out. "He hurt you."

"He did. But, honey, love is messy. It isn't black-and-white or right and wrong. We forgive those we love when they hurt us. Love is the sum of all our actions, not just one, and not just when it's easy or perfect."

"Are you going back to him?"

"Heavens, no. But I forgave him. Isn't it time you do too?"

His stomach pitched and rolled. He just didn't understand. His father had turned their lives upside down. Marsh had gone from idolizing him to hating him in the blink of an eye. He had been there to comfort his mother through the days of the divorce. He had listened to her cry herself to sleep when she thought he couldn't hear her.

"You've got to let go of the hate."

"How can you even say that?"

"Everything was always so black and white with you. It's admirable. But, there are shades of gray. You've always seen me as a victim."

"You were a victim."

"But I'm not anymore."

"I'm just not sure I understand why—"

"You really want me to explain the birds and the bees to you?"

Now it was Marsh's turn to flush. But that sick feeling in the pit of his stomach wouldn't go away. He didn't understand. He couldn't forgive his father.

"I refuse to end up like the judge," he said fiercely.

"You are not Bobby. You are never going to have the same negative behavior as him. You're not a cheater. But, not all of your father is bad. He can be generous, and kind, and a good friend." His mother grabbed his hand and squeezed his fingers, her skin dry and papery against his rougher callused fingers. "You're never going to be able to move on unless you find a way to forgive him."

Marsh shoved his chair away from the table and snatched his hands from his mother's. "I can't do that."

His mother stood. "Marsh—"

He made a show of glancing at his watch. "I've got to go. I've got a meeting."

Marsh left quickly, not wanting to fight with his mother. But he didn't actually need to meet Ayesha for another hour, so he checked in with the office.

"Hey, any information on the hospitals and finding the guy who attacked Ayesha?"

"Well, hello to you too," Kita snarked at him. "What bug crawled up your butt?"

Marsh sighed. "I just talked my mother."

"Oh. Rough."

As he got into his car, he glanced over at Kita's childhood home next to his. She should understand why he couldn't forgive his father. Right?

Kita said, "Actually, yeah, I was just about to call you. I found a patient intake at one of the hospitals."

"What have you got?"

"Still working on getting the patient data. Hopefully in the next few hours."

AYESHA PACED around the confines of her loft, annoyed with herself and yet unable to quell her nerves. She smoothed her damp palms down the short minidress with a flirty skirt. Her heels were laser-sharp stilettos. She grabbed a pashmina and wrapped it around herself, then removed her long wool churchgoing coat from the closet.

She didn't do dress-up. Most days she was doing well if she put on a bra. Holey jeans and oversized chambray shirts splattered with paint were her norm. And frankly what she preferred.

Why the hell had she agreed to go out to dinner with him anyway? She looked longingly at her unfinished canvas.

She'd been painting furiously since he was here this morning. Thoughts of Marsh Adams had dominated her brain, and the half-finished result was sexy, erotic and some of her best work.

Half-finished being the most important part. She should stay at home and paint. The show of her lifetime was coming up fast and the gallery owner had been pressuring her for the last two canvases.

If his firm was going to do her public relations, what did he need her for?

She went from stomping to pacing to stomping. At a few minutes after five her cell rang. "Yeah?"

"Sorry I'm late. I'm outside."

There was a sharp rap at her door. Ayesha startled, nearly tripping on her shaggy carpet.

She walked to the door and peered through the security peephole. Even distorted in the fish lens shape of the glass, he was attractive. More than attractive.

She yanked open the door. "Let's go."

He didn't say a word, just nodded. Together they left her

building. When they got to the entrance, he frowned at the broken lock. "I don't like that that's still broken."

She wasn't crazy about it either. But he wasn't her keeper. "It needs a special lock. They're coming tomorrow."

He led her to a late model Mercedes. Black and sleek with leather seats and a leather-wrapped steering wheel. It was cold enough outside that there was a nip in the air.

She slid into the sedan and gave a little shudder. The leather seats and old money vibe reminded her far too much of her childhood.

"I've got the basic outline of the plan." Marsh took off into traffic, driving competently and not looking at her. "We can review it over dinner."

Twenty minutes later they entered a trendy little Italian place in a trendy neighborhood filled with trendy people. Of which she was not.

MARSH HELD out Ayesha's chair and she looked at him steadily before shrugging and sitting down.

"I can't be a gentleman?"

"I'm sure you can. The question is why would you?" She shook out her napkin and picked up the menu.

Apparently, he'd completely lost his touch. And he wasn't about to tell her that he loved her sexiness.

"Still not sure what we're doing here."

"This restaurant has a reputation for tipping off paparazzi to famous diners."

"I'm not famous."

She was being modest. His research had dug up that she was quite the up-and-coming artist. And with her family connections, she had occasionally been in the paper on the society page.

But he wasn't about to stroke her ego. "They aren't going to be calling about you."

She quirked a brow. "You're famous?"

Before he could say more, his father walked into the restaurant. Shit. The last person he wanted to see was the judge. Marsh could hope that his father wouldn't notice them, but he knew that was futile.

The judge cased every single restaurant when he went inside, looking for people he knew, people he'd helped, and those who still owed him a favor. He always worked a room more like a politician than a lawyer.

Marsh saw the exact moment when his father realized he and Ayesha were at the restaurant.

A large smile spread over his father's face. And a pang hit Marsh in the chest. He had not seen such a look of acceptance and pleasure on his father's face in twenty years.

His father strode up to the table and pressed his palm over Marsh's shoulder. He wanted to shrug away from that touch, but he was still lost in that moment of pleasure where he'd been happy to see his father.

"Nice to see you here." The judge turned to Marsh's companion and his brows crimped in a frown. "Ayesha?"

"Nice to see you again, Uncle Bobby."

"What are you doing here…together?"

It was none of his father's business. And he couldn't help needling his father and Ayesha. "Trying to convince her that she needs a bodyguard."

"Not a chance." She laughed but Marsh could hear the edge beneath her voice. "But I never turn down a free meal."

The judge smiled but there was a tenseness around his mouth that had Marsh stiffening. "As long as it's not a date."

"I'm not good enough for her?" Marsh couldn't help but ask harshly.

Ayesha placed her palm over the judge's forearm gently. "Marsh is just giving me some advice, Uncle Bobby."

That was a new one. The prickly grumpy artist had turned conciliatory and placating.

Before his father could say anything else, Lincoln Brown entered the restaurant. Perfect. This probably couldn't get any more awkward.

The old man shuffled up to their table, his gait a little uneven. This time Marsh watched the interaction between Lincoln Brown and his father. There was an easy camaraderie but also an odd tension between the two.

"What are you doing here?" Lincoln Brown addressed his granddaughter.

Ayesha sighed. "Not eating apparently."

Marsh snorted. Nice not to be on the receiving end of that snarkiness.

"So you're listening to reason?" Lincoln Brown said.

Even Marsh could have told the old man that that was the wrong way to handle his granddaughter.

"I'm listening to my stomach." She shot Marsh an annoyed frown. "Did you know they were going to be here?"

"Not a chance." For the moment they were in complete agreement that the old men needed to leave.

Silence as they shared a look.

Apparently they'd left both of the men speechless.

"Come on, Linc, let's go have our dinner."

But as the older men went to their table, Marsh noted the photographer outside the window. He'd requested this particular table, knowing that it would make a good photo op for whomever was lurking around waiting to catch some minor celebrity having dinner out. Great. Chances were that tomorrow's photo would be of the four of them. Still PR but not what Marsh had been attempting.

He sighed.

"What's wrong now?"

"Paparazzi at twelve o'clock."

"And we care why?"

"It was step one in the Adams-Larsen plan to get you some publicity."

AYESHA WAS COMPLETELY EXASPERATED with both her dinner companion and the old men. "I'm not a celebrity."

"Not yet." His voice was low and confident. As if he thought she might be one day.

She shuddered. She didn't ever want to be a celebrity. She just wanted to have a successful show so that if her grandfather ended up in prison she could help with the lawyer's bills. But she certainly couldn't tell Marsh Adams that.

"What's that supposed to mean?"

"It will be in the paper tomorrow that you were having dinner with Marsh Adams of the very exclusive PR company Adams-Larsen, and that you have an exhibition coming up."

Publicity for the show was definitely a good thing. But she was stuck on his tagline for this nonexistent photo. "You're famous?"

"No. But we occasionally use the paps to get press. Now and again, we give them tidbits on people who are actually famous or newsworthy, and then they will take a photo of someone when we request it and get it in the paper."

"And you requested this?"

"Our head PR woman did, yeah."

Head PR woman? "I did some research on you, you know."

His lips lifted in a little smirk and he raised one eyebrow. "And?"

"Yeah. There's been a lot of controversy surrounding your PR firm." She put PR firm in air quotes. "Don't you think it's rather suspicious that with all the speculation about what you really do, that all of the sudden you're announcing your clients?"

"We've decided to take a more open approach to our clientele as long as they're agreeable."

"Why have I been chosen to be the inaugural client that you suddenly decide to out?"

"We've had some issues lately…."

She snorted. "You mean bad publicity."

"There's no such thing as bad publicity." Which was true if you were actually a PR company. However, she wasn't convinced that his company didn't have a hidden side to their business.

"So you're suddenly going to start outing your clients?"

"Only if they let us. We're changing our business model." He didn't appear to like the idea and Ayesha had to wonder why. "The publicity will be good for your show. Is there something special about this particular show?"

She paused, then said, "We're showcasing some new up-and-coming artists as well. This is their big break and I won't do anything to sabotage their chance for exposure."

"Getting publicity for the lead artist should hardly sabotage the other artists."

"Shouldn't you ask me if I'm agreeable?"

"Do you want publicity or not?" His exasperation bled through his words.

She did. She was stuck needing it in case her grandfather did end up in jail. But she didn't want to need it and the reality that she did chafed. Ugh. She just wanted to make her art and be left alone.

"If it's really a problem, we can come up with another way." But Marsh shook his head. "However, this is the best way to make a big splash in a short amount of time."

"Fine."

Ayesha needed to get her head on straight. Part of being a grown-up was doing things you didn't want to do. However, she wasn't crazy about this exposure to Marsh Adams and she still didn't think Adams-Larsen was actually a PR firm.

She put on her art show persona. Like a disguise, her alter ego was polished, charming, and unflappable. Fortunately, she didn't have to pull out agreeable Ayesha very often.

She inhaled deeply, closed her eyes, and let the breath out slowly.

She opened her eyes and smiled, lifting her lips in a curl that was just socially acceptable enough to fool most people.

"What else do you have planned for publicity?"

Marsh frowned. "What's that?"

"What's what?"

"What are you doing?"

"Conversing?"

"You're being far too agreeable."

Her ire rose. Seriously? "I'm having a conversation with you."

"Be real," he snapped out. "Don't be fake."

"You want me to be my normal grouchy grumpy self?"

"Good point." He looked at her and he sighed. "Just don't be fake with me."

She blinked. He wanted her to be herself? A cold place inside unfurled like a shoot reaching toward the warmth of the sun. He wanted her just the way she was.

"Where'd you learn to smile like that?"

"My parents are ambassadors. Spent my early childhood learning etiquette rules and how to behave in public."

"You're very good at it."

She felt defensive. She could be charming when needed. She just didn't usually expend the effort. She frowned at him and opened her mouth to blast him.

"That's better."

She raised her eyebrows.

"Now that we're on track again, what are your publicity goals?" He sounded like he was reading from a script. However, the question was a good one.

"To sell a crap ton of paintings and make a crap ton of money." How was that for real?

Marsh laughed. "That's succinct."

"Just being honest." For Ayesha it was about so much more than the money. It was also about validation and recognition.

"Thank you." Marsh took a sip of sparkling water. "Tell me more about your show."

"The Promise Gallery focuses exclusively on women artists. This particular show is to showcase women artists of color. The show name is Shade: Discovering Color in a World of Darkness."

"But you're the main draw. That's awesome."

Ayesha flushed. "Someone did their homework." She had big shoes to fill, and an opportunity to advance the work of not just herself but the other artists included in the show. The onus was on Ayesha to draw in big clients.

"What kind of art?"

"Modern with mixed media."

"Mixed?"

"A hybrid of paint and other materials." Art was incredibly personal. She'd always felt as if she didn't belong anywhere. Her identity trapped between her mother's ideal of what a daughter should be and a father who was somehow discouraging without ever saying a disparaging word. She'd been too awkward. Too artistic. Too rebellious. And she'd disappeared into art as a way to escape.

Except even that hadn't pleased her mother.

Nowadays she lived to please herself and no one else.

Marsh shifted in his seat as if he could hear her uncomfortable thoughts, but he looked genuinely interested. "What's your why?"

"What is with the self-help bullshit?" Ayesha shot back, uncomfortable with the question. She wasn't about to share her childhood issues with him. "What's *your why?*"

"To help at-risk, vulnerable people."

"Well you're out of luck. I ain't vulnerable."

But she wondered what at-risk people had to do with publicity. She tilted her head and studied him.

He pulled a single sheet of paper out of a portfolio and slid it across the table. "Here's what we've got set up so far." He folded his hands together and threaded his fingers. "It's preliminary and we will add more as we tailor the marketing to tie into your show name. Unfortunately, because the show is so soon, we can't get any magazine coverage, even the online features are scheduled months out, but I'm hoping we might be able to get a spot in the Sunday style section."

So maybe he really did do PR, but somehow she

doubted it. Ayesha read through the details. It was mostly a list of promo options, without the specific details, but still decently comprehensive. News outlets, Facebook, Instagram, Pinterest, holiday shopping tie-ins, which was why the opening was right before Christmas. "You did all this today?"

"Actually our head of PR put this together."

"Then why are you meeting with me?"

"I'm doing this as a favor for a family friend." He pointed to the social media section.

She winced. Social media gave her the hives even if she did think it was a necessary evil.

"She can post for you if you don't want to do it. According to her analysis, you're intermittent at best."

Her need to be authentic warred with her abhorrence of putting all the details of her life online. Did she really want to be that visible?

"Social media is important." But he had a look on his face like he was equally distrustful of it.

"Okay," she said grudgingly.

They ate dinner, exchanging small talk. The kind of shit that bored her silly. She couldn't stand it any longer. "So why don't you get along with your father?"

"Big fan of the judge, are you?" Marsh said.

"He's a good man—"

Marsh snorted, interrupting her defense of his father. "Not really."

"He's a judge. He helps people." He'd helped her Gramps years ago and now they were friends. He had a core of goodness inside him who viewed all people as individuals no matter the color of their skin. He was a good guy. Flawed, for sure, but still a good guy.

"He helps himself," he said through gritted teeth.

"He's your father. You must know why he got into the law."

"So he could wield power over whomever he wanted to?"

Jesus, he was cynical. The exact opposite of his father, who was the ultimate idealist. "It's a wonder he actually raised you."

"He didn't raise me. My mother did."

"You never spent any time with him? He's all about justice."

"Yeah and banging everyone he can."

Ayesha was quiet. She remembered the conversation she had with Bobby Adams years ago. Would Marsh care?

"He once told me…that he hoped the good he did in the courtroom balanced out his failures personally."

Marsh looked taken aback. "Seriously?"

"He knows he didn't always make the best choices."

"Pretty much doesn't care who he hurts."

"He hurt you?"

Marsh Adams shook his head vehemently. "My mother. He hurt my mother."

She could see the truth. His father had hurt him as well. "Haven't you ever done something that you regret? Something you wish you could take back?"

He looked as if he had swallowed a bad clam. "Yeah." Marsh took another gulp of club soda. "And I'm trying to make it better. Unlike the judge who keeps repeating the same pattern over and over and over again."

"So you think you're better than him?"

He looked like he had a sour stomach.

Marsh's cell phone rang. The waiter gave him a dirty look. But when he glanced at the screen, he said, "I have to take this."

MARSH HAD NEVER in his life been happier to have a phone call interrupt a conversation. He was trying to atone for the mistakes he'd made regarding Brianna. And Ayesha's words uncurled a ribbon of shame within him. He had made mistakes. Big ones. He hated that she was calling him out on it. It was far easier to continue to judge his father without judging himself.

"Adams."

"I've got a line on the intruder." Kita didn't bother with hello.

"That's great." He shot a glance at Ayesha and wondered if he could keep the information from her.

Her gaze narrowed on him.

"Where is he?"

"Your girl burned him pretty good." He heard the admiration in Kita's voice and he still felt compelled to defend her.

"He was there to hurt her."

"I got that." Kita listed off the hospital and floor where the guy was a patient.

"Do you have a name?"

"Yes, and I'm running it as we speak."

"Okay, great. Thank you."

"You want me to go check him out?"

Before he could answer, Ayesha put her hand on Marsh's arm. Electricity zinged through his body, blasting away his common sense. "I want to go with you."

"Is that our new client?"

The amusement in Kita's voice threw him off. "Yes."

"You should take her with you."

"Why's that?"

"It's clearly not a random attack. It's possible when you ask the questions, she'll catch something that you miss."

"She's not trained."

"She's not an idiot, is she?"

"Of course not."

"Take me with you," Ayesha reiterated.

"Okay. Thanks." Marsh hung up with Kita.

"Oh thank God, can we get out of here?"

Marsh eyed her fancy dress and heels. "We haven't finished dinner."

"I don't care. We can get it to go."

"As you wish." Within a few minutes, they had takeout containers for their pasta and Marsh had paid the bill. Once they were in the car and heading to the hospital, he said, "I'm asking the questions. You are just there to listen."

"I thought your friend said I might have good information." She propped her fist on her hip and cocked her head.

Marsh definitely preferred this assertive woman with attitude to the weird smiling accommodating one at the beginning of dinner.

"Just follow my lead."

A few minutes later they parked at the hospital and went up to the sixth floor, where her assailant had been admitted. Marsh peeked into his room. The upper half of the guy's face was wrapped in bandages.

"Who's there?" The guy's voice was shaky as he lay in the hospital bed. He was little more than a kid.

"We'd like to ask you some questions." Marsh didn't identify them, and the guy couldn't see, so they might get a few answers before he clammed up. "I'm here to talk about the attack."

"Yes, I was attacked. Are you a cop?"

"I was talking about you attacking a woman in her home."

"I don't know what you're talking about."

"Quit lying," Marsh said. "We know you attacked a woman in her loft."

"You can't prove that," he said boldly.

They might not be able to but at this point they needed information more than they needed him to be detained by the cops. "What did you have against her?"

"I don't know anyone who might have been attacked."

"Then why did you do it."

"Not saying I did."

"Can we cut through this bullshit?" Ayesha snarled.

The guy in the bed stiffened and shrank away from her. "Is that her?"

She demanded, "Why did you want to hurt me?"

"I didn't," he whimpered.

Marsh didn't think the kid was lying. If anything, he seemed afraid of Ayesha. "Then who did want to hurt her?"

"Why should I tell you?"

"Because it's your civic duty."

"What's in it for me?"

"Seriously?" Ayesha's annoyance was clear. "You go into somebody's home and attack them and you think you're entitled to get something out of it?"

"Look, we just want to know who hired you," Marsh said evenly and shot Ayesha a look. *Shut up,* he mouthed at her.

She bristled but didn't open her mouth.

"Who hired you?" Marsh said again in a hard voice.

"I don't know."

Ayesha snorted.

"Who hired you?"

"I will kick your ass if you don't tell us," Ayesha threatened.

Marsh rolled his eyes. Although the kid was clearly afraid of her.

"Tell. Us," she demanded.

The kid shrank away from her. "Seriously. I don't know. I don't know! I got the job on the dark web."

"Website?" Marsh snapped out.

The kid pressed his lips together obstinately.

"Here's another one. How'd you get paid?"

"I only got half since I was injured. I've got medical bills to pay. Bills you are responsible for." The kid turned his head toward Ayesha, even though they knew he couldn't see them.

Unbelievable. The kid was trying to extort money. Finally, Marsh put a twenty in the kid's hand. Ayesha was livid. But then the kid started talking.

"Bitcoin."

Potentially traceable but extremely difficult to execute.

"You really don't know who hired you?"

"Nope."

"What was the website?"

"I'm gonna need more money for that."

Marsh slapped another twenty in the kid's hand.

Finally he rattled off a site Marsh had never heard of but he made a note. He'd have Kita get on it. "What were you hired to do?"

"I was just supposed to scare her." The guy grimaced. "Instead, I'm all fucked up."

"Cry me a river," Ayesha said. "You got everything you need?"

"No more questions." Marsh leaned closer to the man. "You are incredibly lucky that she hasn't pressed charges."

The kid sneered as if somehow more comfortable now that the questions were over.

"Yet."

His smirk disappeared.

"Know this, if you go after her again, I will find you and make you sorry." Marsh whispered, "I know everything about you. Where you live, where you bank, where you hang out."

The kid cowered in the hospital bed.

"If the person who hired you contacts you, I want to know about it." Marsh dropped his card on the little table next to his hospital bed.

"S-sure."

"No conveniently forgetting or we will be back to make you sorry."

"Okay. Okay."

Marsh nodded once decisively. "Now we're done."

Chapter 8

They were headed away from the hospital. Ayesha was quiet. Thinking about the fact that this random kid had accepted money to scare her. And while he was lying in that bed, saying he hadn't been going to hurt her, she remembered the menace that she felt from him last night. He might not have been paid to hurt her, but he'd been thinking about it.

She wanted to fall apart, her insides quaking. Last night had a positive ending but the outcome could have been horribly different. She tightened her fists to stop her body from shaking as the ramifications cascaded through her brain.

Luckily the little asshole hadn't had any permanent damage to his eyesight. But damn him for breaking her safety barrier and making her worry about her security.

Marsh Adams had been uncharacteristically quiet too.

"Can you just drop me at home?" She had so much left to do. When she'd gone to dinner hours ago, she had only carved out two hours from her production schedule. Now she was really behind.

Traffic was heavier than usual, probably due to the holidays. The lampposts were festively decorated with wreaths and fake candles. White lights twinkled in the trees that lined the streets, and storefronts were decorated for the holidays with plenty of garland and tinsel and bling. She didn't have time to savor the holidays, it didn't go with her tough girl image anyway. She'd perfected that image years ago to hide her vulnerability, but she loved everything about Christmas. Just thinking about the holiday gave her a warm fuzzy feeling. Even if she did have a billion things to do.

"You can't stay there."

"*Can't?*" That got her blood going, and that happy feeling evaporated. "First, you don't tell me what to do. Second, it's my home and I have no intention of leaving it."

"Unless your management has fixed the lock on the door while we were at dinner, it's not safe."

Her heart gave a pang. Someone had hired a man to scare her. That had put all her neighbors in jeopardy. They'd contacted the management company and were waiting for a locksmith to fix the door but unfortunately the guy had damaged the doorjamb, and it wasn't as simple as putting in a new lock.

But all of that was none of his damn business. "Well, thanks for that update."

"I'm trying to protect you."

She could hear the censure in his voice, as if she should just shut up and accept his help. "I didn't say I wanted protection." As a matter of fact, the reason she'd gone to dinner was because they were supposed to talk about public relations.

"Look," he said tiredly. He drove with a quiet confidence, his left wrist draped over the wheel, his right hand tapping the center console as if he were unaware of the movement. "Your place isn't safe. Do you have someone you can stay with? Your grandfather maybe?"

She didn't want to acknowledge that he was right. "I have a show to get ready for." Even if she did have someone to go stay with, she couldn't leave her condo. Her studio and the last two paintings were there. Again, none of his damn business. "I want to stay in my own place."

"You can come stay with me. I have a guest room."

"I'm not your responsibility."

"The old man and your grandfather will kill me if anything happens to you."

"Well, that's your problem, not mine."

"Ayesha." The entreaty in his voice stopped her. He wasn't being arrogant, and he wasn't being difficult, he really was worried about her.

She would admit to herself that she was a little rattled to spend the night in her condo alone, especially after listening to that punk talk about scaring her. She relented and confessed the true reason she was staying put.

"I have to finish my paintings." This show was important. It was supposed to take her to the next level. Important collectors were coming. And if the thought of having to socialize with them made her skin crawl, she would do it anyway and put on her nicest, fakest smile and get through it. Just to prove that she was good enough. That she had what it took to be a recognized artist. She had been lucky to get this show and she couldn't blow this opportunity. She'd been working for the last five years, slowly building a clientele and her reputation. She couldn't flake on her responsibilities now. If she did, she might never have this opportunity again. Not to mention that Promise Lewis, the gallery owner, and the other four women in the show were counting on her. "I have to finish."

"I have a solution." Marsh rubbed his finger along the steering wheel. "But I don't think you'll like it."

"Try me. You never know unless you ask." She giggled. Her grams had said that to her when she was growing up and it was a motto she lived by faithfully. It was part of the reason she was where she was. Because she asked.

"What if I stay at your condo?" He started speaking quickly. "You have that big sofa. You can work and I will nap but be there if someone else comes along to try and harm you."

"That seems very…in character for you."

"Someone needs to protect you." He shrugged his wide shoulders, the breadth enough to keep her safe. "Why not me?"

She thought about how much she had to do. About how she had lost the last day and half, first mooning over the man next to her and then worrying about everything from the break-in to her grandfather's problems. "Okay," she said softly.

"I promise not to bother you. I won't interrupt your painting. I'll make myself as scarce as possible."

"I said okay."

"Yeah, but I can tell you don't really mean it."

She rolled her eyes. "I said *okay*."

And that was how she ended up with a houseguest—a distracting, sexy, protector— watching her work.

MARSH HAD GOTTEN COMFORTABLE. He'd taken off his sport coat and removed his shoes. He lounged on her sofa and pretended not to watch her work as he watched her work.

In the past thirty-six hours he had turned into a complete creeper.

He'd followed her, stalked her, staked out her condo, and now he was even closer and watching her work. She painted with her whole body. It was mesmerizing and tantalizing. After they'd come home from dinner and the hospital, she'd gone into her bedroom and closed the door sharply. A few minutes later, she'd emerged in a pair of tight leggings and another one of those oversized shirts splattered with paint, buttoned just enough to preserve her modesty and yet open far enough that a hint of her cleavage teased his vision.

Once again, she wasn't wearing a bra.

Marsh kept his groan to himself and grabbed the throw over the end of the sofa so that his semi-hard erection wasn't visible. The last thing he wanted to do was make her uncomfortable. His longing was not her problem. But damn, did he want her.

Marsh scanned the open floorplan of her loft.

The main room was a mixture of exposed brick, industrial metal lights and accents, and plastered walls painted a pure white. The kitchen area was around a corner in an L shape. One long counter held the sink and oven range, while the short end of the L had the refrigerator and glass-fronted cabinets holding plain white dishes. A short island had a counter overhang and two bar stools for a place to eat in. Across from the island was a door that led to her bedroom and bathroom. The slightly ajar door revealed an unmade queen bed with white sheets and a black comforter. Pillows in gray were scattered across the comforter as if she'd flung them aside.

Marsh tore his gaze from the bedroom. Nothing to see here.

Instead he returned to watching her paint.

She appeared to be working on two different canvases, both in mid painting. Bright lights with a warm glow illuminated her work area while the rest of the living space was shrouded in shadows. Once she got down to work, her focus was laser sharp. He was pretty sure she had forgotten he was there. Which suited him just fine. The opportunity to observe her work was good.

She stood back from a large canvas at least four by six feet, her head tilted as she studied the interesting slashes and squiggles. He thought it was a couple. Lovers, perhaps. Twined together and lounging on something. Though the painting was abstract, the forms conveyed a sensuality and a passion that practically leapt off the canvas. He shifted on the sofa and let his thoughts drift drowsily.

She had been lost in creating for hours.

She put her hands on the small of her back and arched toward the ceiling. Her elbows were akimbo and her hair flew around her face as she sighed gustily.

She swept her arms over her head and pressed her palms together, then pulled them in prayer position to her chest. She folded at the waist and bent over. Her loose shirt billowed around her as she held her head at her knees. The tops of her gorgeous, bare breasts plumped out of the V and Marsh fought the urge to groan.

"Jesus, I can hear you thinking from over here." She took a step back and turned to face him. "What?"

"I like it."

"My life is complete," she snapped.

"It's a couple, right?"

Her brows rose. "Yeah."

"It's very…sensual." He wasn't an art critic. He didn't know the right words. But he did know what he liked. And he loved that painting.

"That's what I was aiming for."

"It's very modern."

"I like the ambiguity of abstract art." She was sharing, which he loved. "I like that the work is open to interpretation. That everyone can take away something different. Still be touched by it, but no two people will be touched in the same way."

"In my line of work, ambiguity isn't a positive," he said reflectively.

Ayesha bristled. "Maybe it should be."

Jesus she was prickly. "I'm more of a black-and-white person."

"So I've heard."

With those three words, she stopped him cold. "You've heard?"

"Sure. Your father talks about you all the time."

The judge talked about him? That was downright weird.

"You look surprised." She dipped the brush she'd been working with in the jar of linseed oil. The same stuff she'd thrown at the intruder. Marsh knew she wouldn't throw it at him, but he still didn't want to piss her off.

"Uncle Bobby talks about you all the time. He's very proud of you, you know."

Marsh snorted. Doubtful.

"But he's very aware of your faults."

Faults? "What faults?" His father was the one who had major personality defects. Of course, he'd just come off the mess of trusting Brianna Walsh.

"You're rigid." She ticked off on her fingers. Her long, elegant, paint-stained fingers. "And apparently you refuse to forgive him."

He couldn't believe his father had been talking about him.

"It seems very weird that you know so much about me, when I know nothing about you."

"I'm an open book."

Now that was a lie. He had only known her a day and a half and already he knew that she had secrets inside her. And he knew that discovering those secrets would be a hunt. A treasure hunt to find her depths, to know her, and that whoever persevered would be one lucky bastard. Until she opened her mouth.

"Yeah, right."

"There is that black and white again." She had looked for a moment as if she might confide in him. But that moment had slipped away, and he couldn't help but mourn its loss.

He shouldn't even be thinking about her that way. The last time he'd been led around by his dick, bad things had happened. She'd been lying to him since they met. And he had no frame of reference as to whether they were little lies or big lies. The only thing worse than a liar was someone who was a liar and a criminal.

AYESHA NEEDED A BREAK. Just a small one. She was exhausted after her mostly sleepless last night and the past few hours of nonstop painting. She sauntered to the sofa and sat down on the opposite end.

The amusement that had lit his brown eyes a few minutes ago had disappeared. Now he was frowning. Since his mood had shifted, she figured she'd ask, "You said earlier he let you down." She wanted to know. Because the truth was her Gramps had let her down too. And though she loved him with every fiber of her being, his actions had hurt her. "How did you get past it?"

"You ask as if you have a similar problem," Marsh said.

Ayesha rocked her head but didn't answer. This was as vulnerable as she got. And if she wasn't so tired, she probably wouldn't have brought it up.

"I don't think I can get past it." His body language was closed off, shuttered. His arms crossed over his chest, and his chin tucked down. He didn't *want* to get past it. Before she could reply, he said, "He doesn't deserve my forgiveness." But something in his gaze was bewildered. "I don't understand how my mother ever got over it."

"I know he regrets how he treated her." That seemed to be the wrong thing to say because he stiffened.

"And how would you know that?"

"Because he told me. Because he said the greatest gift he'd ever gotten was your mother's forgiveness. And he liked to think that all the other good he had done in his life balanced out that one act of betrayal."

"Yeah," Marsh said cynically. "I'm guessing he uses that line to get women into bed."

That wasn't why he'd told her. But Ayesha was going to keep that to herself.

"Besides, you'd have to have been betrayed to even understand." He made the proclamation as if he had a lock on disappointment, and their small moment of connection had been broken. Whatever. She leaned against the sofa, her neck resting along the back as she stared up at the ceiling.

"I'll let you get back to it."

"I need a break." She gathered her composure around her. "Just for a minute."

EXHAUSTION COATED HER FEATURES. Her makeup had long since worn off, and shadows darkened the skin beneath her beautiful hazel eyes. Stress had carved lines around her mouth, emphasizing her lips, drawing him as he remembered that kiss.

Ayesha's eyes drifted closed.

"Why don't you take a short nap?"

"No time," she said. But she hadn't opened her eyes, and a little sigh of breath left her as she drifted slightly to the side.

Marsh wanted to gather her in his arms and have her rest on him. To use him as her safe harbor. To let him protect her. But she would never allow that. When she was quiet and her guard was lowered, he could see the exhaustion on her face.

He shifted, propping his back against the arm of the sofa, keeping quiet and letting her rest, content to sit in silence and watch over her.

Light seared his eyeballs, penetrating his closed eyelids and stabbing into his brain. Something soft shifted next to him as he tried to wade up from the depths of sleep. His bed seemed extra hard, but a soft pillow cradled his head. He wrapped his arms around the pillow and snuggled back in for more sleep, wishing he'd remembered to close his blinds.

The scent of chemicals and a slight musk tickled his nose. The pillow beneath his cheek was supple and warm. Other things penetrated his consciousness slowly. He'd been having a most erotic dream.

Ayesha had been painting naked.

Other sensations crowded in. His morning erection was cradled by someone, a warm body pressed against his. Marsh cracked open his eyes slightly, wincing at the brightness streaming in through the industrial windows. How the hell did she stand all this light?

His arms were full of sexy woman. She was clearly still asleep. He was fuzzy on how they ended up wrapped together as if they had been lovers for years instead of slightly adversarial acquaintances. As if his body knew hers. Her gorgeously unruly hair tickled his nose. She rubbed her ass against his growing erection, and his cock was on board with her moves.

He needed to extricate himself before she woke up. Leaning into her body, he rubbed his nose gently along the line of her neck and placed a kiss behind her ear. His arms were wrapped around her body, one around her waist and one across her collarbone. At the innocent kiss she arched her body and pressed her breast into his palm. She was perfect. Her beaded nipple teased his palm, and he was helpless to do anything less than squeeze.

She moaned at the light caress and reached behind her to thread her fingers through his hair. Her legs moved restlessly when he slid his hand inside her shirt and cupped her skin, plucking at her nipple and rolling the sharp bud between his thumb and forefinger. She turned over to face him. And he stopped, coming fully awake.

Consent was necessary. He was awake enough now to realize that he needed to back away. She slipped her hand beneath his untucked shirt and scraped her nails up his back. She pressed kisses against the bare skin of his chest exposed by his partially unbuttoned shirt.

"Ayesha." He was desperate for her to wake up.

Her eyes popped open and she blinked wide. She pulled away from him. He was rock hard, his body ready to go. But he knew as soon as awareness filtered through her that this forbidden intimacy would disappear.

She froze. They were so close he could see the flecks of other colors in her hazel gaze—blue, green, brown and gold glittered, her pupils were blown, and her short thick black lashes were curled tight.

She had stopped breathing. He lifted his hands from her shoulders as if in surrender. There was nothing he could do about his cock prodding her belly, but he wanted to make sure that she in no way felt trapped.

"I'm not sure how we ended up this way."

She blinked again and he waited, wondering if she was going to blast him for touching her.

She snickered. Not the response he was expecting. "You're a little old to need a lesson on sex ed."

But oh would he love for her to teach him.

"I sat down for a minute to rest. We were talking and I must have fallen asleep." She hadn't pushed away from him. "I was cold."

He still wasn't sure how that they got from her asleep sitting next to him, to them twined together.

"And you're hot." She snickered again. "Apparently I'm like a heat-seeking missile."

"I'll get up." He flushed.

"Seems to me you already are."

"True story." He smiled and began the process of disentangling.

"Wait."

Wait?

Her hand lazily trailed up the skin of his back. "This is…nice."

Now he was the one to bristle. "No guy wants to be called nice." And he wasn't. Not at all.

She used her hands to explore his body, kissing the bare

skin at the V of his shirt as she tested his muscles and smoothed her hands along his skin.

She glanced over at her half-finished painting. "Life imitates art." She swirled her tongue over his skin.

"I like art." He was amazed at the breathless tone of his voice.

"I like life better," she said.

"I can't do this. I can't get involved with a client." He couldn't. The last thing he needed to do was get tangled up with her. He was still trying to redeem himself from the last time he'd gotten involved with a client.

"I'm not talking about involved. I'm talking about sex."

"You don't understand."

"You don't want me?"

He nudged her with his cock. "It's obvious that I do."

"Could just be morning wood."

"Don't ever sell yourself short like that. This is for you."

She glanced over at the painting again. She took a deep breath, sighed. "See that canvas?"

"Of course I see it."

"You know what it represents?"

They had discussed this last night. "A couple. Sensual. Passionate."

"Think more personally." She undid the buttons on her shirt. Marsh began to sweat. She was vulnerable. He was vulnerable. Neither of them was in a place to make a decision like this. Although if it was just sex….

"That's you and me," she said when he didn't answer. Did she mean…?

"Yes. I was thinking about you when I painted that."

Marsh swallowed, his resolve crumbling as she gave him a wicked smile. "I'm not in the market for relationship."

She laughed. "Neither am I."

"This is a bad idea," he said desperately. "A really bad idea."

Shit.

"Bad ideas are my specialty." She spread open her paint-splattered shirt, baring her breasts to his gaze.

Her skin was smooth and walnut brown. Her nipples were a dark maroon, the same color scattered in her hair and flowing over the canvas across from them.

His mouth watered. "May I?" He still needed those words of consent.

"Please do."

Marsh bent his head and sucked on her tight nipple, tonguing the bud to the roof of his mouth. She moaned softly in his ear and whispered, "Harder."

He brought his other hand up and cupped her. She responded with unrestrained passion, undulating like the fluid lines on the canvas.

DAMN HER BODY. She hadn't been this attracted to a man in forever.

The mostly finished canvas was some of her best work. He had inspired her—at a point when she was feeling decidedly uninspired and feeling the pressure regarding the import of the show and the impending problems of her grandfather's issues.

She had finished all the smaller works months ago, but she had been procrastinating about the two larger showpieces. The gallery owner had told her that the big pieces needed to make a statement. She was planning on asking for a lot of money for the work.

Promise Lewis had supported Ayesha throughout her

career and she refused to let her down. The pressure and weight of those expectations had been pushing down on her for months.

So when she'd woken in his arms, it felt like the best sort of serendipity. She'd been needing the comfort of touch. And here he was touching her.

She rolled so that Marsh was beneath her.

She sat up, straddling his thighs. He cupped her breasts in his big hands, playing with her nipples and running his finger along the center of her body, tracing her ribs, dipping into her belly button and then sliding his fingers beneath the elastic of her leggings.

He drew in a sharp breath. "No panties?"

She grinned but didn't answer.

"Shit. What is it with you and underwear?"

"It's a sensory thing. The elastic bothers my skin. Lace is scratchy."

His fingers played with her clit and now it was her turn to draw in a swift breath.

"Believe me, I'm not complaining."

Ayesha closed her eyes and rocked into his fingers. He was penetrating her lightly, his middle finger just barely breaching her body while his other fingers squeezed her swollen sex.

"Praise Jesus."

He curled his fingers around her neck and pulled her down for a kiss. His mouth met hers. She wanted to close her eyes, but his were open and watching her intently. The assessing gaze was a complete turn-on. Ayesha fumbled with the buttons of his shirt, needing to be skin to skin.

Neither of them looked away as she rubbed her breasts over his slightly fuzzy chest. His erection pressed against the bare skin of her belly. Marsh let go and hooked his thumbs in her leggings and shoved them down her legs until they were down around her knees. The spandex constricted her legs, allowing her minimal movement. Marsh flipped them so that she lay beneath him and he quickly unbuckled his jeans. She helped him remove his belt and shove his jeans to his thighs. And still, neither of them looked away. The moment was intense, forging a connection that in that moment seemed unbreakable. She needed him. Needed him inside her. The tip of his erection rubbed her belly, a hot drip of pre-come searing her skin.

They needed a condom. She was on the shot. But she still wasn't taking any chances. He nipped at her mouth.

"Wallet."

She pulled his wallet out of his back pocket and fumbled through until she found a single condom. Marsh continued to kiss her, penetrating her mouth with his tongue, invading her as she needed him to invade the rest of her body. She finally got the wrapper torn open and rolled the condom down his length.

Her leggings were at her knees and his jeans rested on his quads as he pushed into her, sliding in to the hilt without any resistance. When the base of his cock pushed against her clit and his balls bounced against her throbbing sex, they both paused.

He broke the kiss, pushed up onto his elbows, straining his biceps as he held his upper body off hers. "You feel amazing."

They were both restricted by their clothing. The intensity of his gaze was too much and she shut her eyes quickly. "Do me."

As if he'd been waiting for permission, he pulled out and then plunged back in. Ayesha gripped his ass in her hands and pushed him hard as they banged into each other, with every rock and thrust pushing her closer to the edge. Their movements were frantic, frenzied, as though, if they didn't come together, they would explode into a ball of firecrackers and float away into a puff of nothingness.

She opened her legs as wide as she could. He pounded between her thighs, the sensations overwhelming. Her tits bounced. His thick cock spread her wide. The constriction of their clothing, his hot skin beneath her palms, and the intense heated look in his eyes coalesced into a ball of need. She hadn't been able to keep her eyes closed, she'd opened them again so she could watch. Watch as his white dick surrounded by a halo of golden curls pushed into her thatch of dark curly hair, the contrast of their skin an erotic reminder of their differences.

"Goddamn, you're incredible.

His thrusts got harder as he did. Ayesha balanced on the edge.

He pushed up and bit her nipple lightly, just on the edge of pain, and she threw herself over the cliff and into the abyss. A long, low wail burst from her as her body convulsed around his cock.

As if he'd been waiting for her, waiting for permission, her orgasm triggered his, and he began to pump into her in hot, hard pulses. Every throb pushed at the walls of her vagina, rubbing her G spot, stimulating her on so many levels. Her mind splintered into fractal light, colors burst behind her eyelids in a display so bright she'd like to commit it to memory. But her thoughts disintegrated, exploding into fragments and leaving her addled and yet satisfied. She collapsed beneath him in a puddle of satisfaction.

This had probably been a mistake. And she didn't give a fuck.

Chapter 9

Marsh was wrecked.

The sex had been earth shattering, life changing. That sense of intimacy as he looked into her eyes —he felt as if she could see all away down into his soul into every dark crevice and misunderstood pocket that he kept hidden from the world. Her piercing gaze had seen it all and still stayed. As if she knew him, and she was okay with him with all his faults and his messes that he was still trying to clean up. But he already knew the second she regained her senses, she would push him away. And he couldn't blame her.

Trust was going to be a hard, slow journey.

He didn't even know why he was contemplating trying to gain her trust except that she stirred something in him. When she pushed off him and headed to the bathroom without a word, the fact that he'd been right still caused a sinking feeling in his stomach.

He hated it when he was right.

Running water from the bathroom penetrated his senses until another noise penetrated.

His cell was ringing. Jill's ringtone.

Shit. While he didn't regret what had just happened, and he didn't believe it would be a problem, his partner wasn't going to see it that way. Marsh sat up on the sofa, his bare ass on the fancy leather and his jeans still strapped around his quads. He grabbed a tissue from the box on the coffee table and disposed of the condom quickly. Then he propped his elbows on his knees and put his head in his hands, rubbing his face, trying to wake up, preparing for the next few moments.

He tugged up his pants and zipped them up, then grabbed his phone and pressed the accept button. "Marsh Adams."

"Hey, good job last night."

Marsh started. He knew she wasn't talking about what had just happened, and still there was a moment of shame before he shoved it away.

"What's up?"

"Small snippet on the society page. We've already had people calling to confirm that Ayesha Brown is a client."

Marsh was more worried about her safety than her publicity because he didn't think the danger had passed. "What did you say?"

"We said no comment. For now. We've got to get her approval to leak her name." Jill was silent for a second. "We probably should've gotten it first, but you said she needed publicity and even if we don't confirm it, this has given her some already. They referenced her upcoming show at The Promise Gallery."

"Okay. We never got around to signing the contract." Marsh was hyperaware of the fact that Ayesha had come out of the bathroom and was standing there giving him a death glare.

"All right. If she agrees, we can tip off the paps again. She should also sign the confidentiality agreement. If she comes into the office, we can discuss the PR in depth." Jill was in her element in her super planning mode, which would've made Marsh happy…except that he was trapped between the professional—Jill's hyper focus on the details—and the personal—the disheveled, still half-dressed woman of this morning's desire.

Ayesha was stunning. And he wanted nothing more than to take her to bed and ravish her some more. But the hands on her hips and the squint of her eyes were a dead giveaway that he wasn't getting anywhere close to her again. At least not this morning.

"Sounds good, Jill. I've got to go. Later." He pressed the off button and waited for it.

"What was that?"

"My partner. There's a small article with a picture identifying you and me and they reference your show. Right now, Adams-Larsen is saying no comment, but I can change that and we can confirm that you are a PR client. If you are amenable."

"Client."

"Yes." He waited patiently. She was a smart woman and she would make her own decisions. He'd already given her the sales pitch last night. It was possible he hadn't really mentioned that it would help out ALIAS but he didn't care.

"We didn't get around to the legalese last night." The phone call regarding her assailant had interrupted. He flushed. He'd managed to get around to all sorts of stuff. Of course, once she signed the contract, she would be totally off limits. She should have been anyway.

Marsh reached for his suit coat, where he had the agreement in his pocket. "As long as you're agreeable and you sign this legal document, I'll have my partner confirm that you're client of ALIAS."

"ALIAS?"

"Yeah, just a cute little acronym for the agency. Adams-Larsen Inc. and Associates."

"But ALIAS doesn't have much to do with publicity, does it?"

Good point.

Marsh avoided the question by pulling the agreement from his pocket. It was a little wrinkled, but it would hold up in a court of law. He pointed to the dotted line. "Sign here."

She raised her eyebrows at him. He was trying not to be distracted by the fact that her shirt was still mostly unbuttoned, showing a swath of smooth and supple walnut-colored skin. He also tried to forget that he had kissed his way down her body until he buried his face in the curls that hid her sex. But it was difficult. Her scent still lingered on him.

"I'm certainly not going to sign it without reading it first. Make yourself at home." Ayesha dropped down onto the sofa as if completely unconcerned with the fact that they just had mind-blowing sex right there. She focused in on the short but succinct contract, clearly reading each line carefully. She chewed on the end of his pen as she studied one sentence and made a small change.

She got to the bottom of the document, hesitated for a moment, then carefully signed on the dotted line. He had expected her signature to be bold and wild like her personality, but she wrote in a small precise script and then handed the paper back to him.

"Now that I'm your client, it would be a great time for you to leave. I have things to do and you'll only be in the way."

And there it was—she was kicking him to the curb.

IT WAS time to get to work.

Marsh had used a good portion of his inheritance to get ALIAS off the ground along with Jillian's severance from the Marshals.

Everyone thought that he had left the US Marshals because of his protector complex. But the truth was the rules had sometimes chafed. And he believed with every fiber of his being that ALIAS provided a service that was necessary and vital to those people in distress who didn't qualify for federal protection. Until he'd fucked up, ALIAS had had a 100% success rate with their relocated clients. They had taken people in danger, obscured their histories and resettled them in new locations. They were safe and he was extremely proud of that record. Even if no one knew what they had done. They worked in secrecy and silence to protect people. It was extremely satisfying and gratifying to know that he had truly helped people.

But then he'd gone and ruined it by getting involved with Brianna Walsh. A criminal who had snowed them all.

He headed to Jill's office. It was bigger than his, which was fine with him. They entertained clients there and it had become the de facto casual congregating place for the staff. Marsh popped his head in to say hello. Kita was sprawled on the love seat, and even though it was ten degrees outside, she only wore her workout gear, booty shorts and a sleeveless spandex tank top. Her straight black hair was up in a ponytail and sweat shimmered on her cheeks as if she'd just come from sparring on the mats in the basement. Jill, on the other hand, was perfectly dressed in her slim almost throwback suit, high-heeled pumps, and her hair up in some sort of fancy girl twist. But what struck Marsh dumb was the smiles on both their faces.

"Come on in." Jill was practically glowing. Her happiness made him happy. But it also opened a hole in his heart. He studied her. She lost her smile. "What's wrong?"

"Not a thing." Marsh dropped into a wing chair and tilted his head, watching Jill. "You're happy."

She hadn't been right after the end of their last case. She'd worked with Hamish Ballard, a slightly annoying Scotsman who Marsh still wasn't sure he trusted. But… "He makes you happy."

"Deliriously."

Kita had changed too. For the better as well.

"Alex makes you happy."

"Well, yeah, when he's not annoying the shit out of me." But Kita laughed and he knew she was mostly kidding.

"How did that happen?"

"It was a difficult process."

Marsh was shocked to realize that he wanted that. That instinctive smile that came before everything else, before every other annoyance and detail. Pretty amazing since he had avoided relationships for so long. But as he contemplated his two best friends, he realized he wanted what they had.

"Any luck on tracing that bitcoin payment?"

"Still working on it. I have a program running that'll send a note to my watch when it's done."

"I've been thinking we should monitor that same site. Since he didn't succeed, it's possible whoever hired him will try to hire someone else."

Kita said, "Already on it."

"Using bitcoin suggests a level of sophistication. But the

attack itself was amateur. The guy was clearly out of his element," Jillian said.

Marsh thought about how Ayesha had kicked the guy's ass. "Or maybe she's just that good."

Kita sat up. "I thought she was an artist?"

"She is. Her work is amazing." Marsh couldn't keep the admiration from his voice. He loved her work. And when he thought about that painting about those two lovers entwined and how they had mimicked the erotic art, he smiled.

"You slept with her, didn't you?" The happiness that had been in Jill's voice was gone. She was…pissed.

"You slept with her?" Kita's voice rose, along with her eyebrows.

"No one said that." Marsh hedged.

"Oh my God. You did."

"I stayed at her condo and watched over her."

"While she was underneath you?" Jill bit out.

Marsh flushed. "Jesus, Jill."

"I thought you were trying to fix this."

"I am. That's why we now have a new client." He pulled the crumpled contract from his pocket.

"Looks like you slept on it," Kita said.

Okay so he had fallen asleep with it in his pocket.

"It was just to let off steam," Marsh said. He didn't want to say it but the truth was "It was mostly her at her request." Except that didn't come out right. "She is rattled. She's an artist and the entire situation is out of her experience."

"And you know that for sure?" Jill said. "The reality is we don't know enough about her. She could be playing you."

Jill was saying all the things he had considered himself. "But I don't think so."

"And that worked out so well last time."

Jill was right.

Marsh countered, "I'm keeping an eye on her."

"I'm still running background. Do you know her grandparents were officially given guardianship of her when she was in her early teens? That seems a little odd, doesn't it?"

Marsh's temper began to rise. "About as odd as someone coming to live at their best friend's house when they're seventeen."

Now it was Kita's turn to flush. "Point taken. But it still deserves a little more digging. Her parents aren't dead. And the fact that they officially transferred guardianship to her father's parents is unusual."

It was. Marsh turned off the endorphins-crazed part of his brain and began considering other angles. "Anything else in her background from when she was a minor?"

"If there is, it's sealed tight. I haven't found anything. A few little idiosyncrasies in her middle school record. But everyone acts out in middle school. It sucks."

Unless it showed a pattern of behavior. But then there would have been something in her adult life. Right?

Jill softened her voice. "Look Marsh, I'm not saying that she's hiding something. I'm just saying watch your back."

MARSH WAS BACK where he didn't want to be…at the judge's office. He nodded to the receptionist. She was sputtering again. But Marsh ignored her. He rapped once hard on the door and opened it again.

The judge wasn't alone.

However, just like the last time, Lincoln Brown was in the office.

What was going on with that? This was literally three days in a row that his father and the elder Brown were thick as thieves.

"Marsh!" His father's smile was shaky, and the surprise on his face caused a weird pang of regret in Marsh's chest.

"What's wrong?" His bigger-than-life father was looking frail. Smaller.

"I'm just becoming more aware of my own mortality."

"What brought this on?"

"Getting older sucks." Lincoln Brown interrupted their tense exchange. "And when something from your past smacks you in the face, you have regrets all over again."

"He doesn't care about all that." His father waved away Lincoln's concerns. "What can I do for you?"

"Well, since you're both here, I can ask you at the same time." Marsh dropped into the chair across from his father's massive desk. He propped his elbows on the arms and pushed his legs out straight and then crossed them at the ankles. He threaded his fingers together. "What's really going on with Ayesha?"

"Did something happen?" The expression on Lincoln Brown's face was fearful, anxious.

"Is she okay?" His father asked.

Both men were stressed, upset, but not surprised.

"I want to know more about this threat." Marsh made his voice hard. But instead of crumbling, both men seem to straighten.

"Your job is to make sure no harm comes to her," his father said.

"It's difficult to do that when I have no idea where the threat is coming from."

"A former…business associate of mine threatened Ayesha."

"How?" Marsh started compiling a mental dossier of facts.

"Verbally," her grandfather said.

"Why not go to the police?"

"First of all, no one would believe me. He carries quite a bit of influence."

"Why did he threaten her?"

"Because he wants me to do something for him." Lincoln Brown shook his head. "I refused."

The judge interrupted. "I was hoping that after dinner last night…" But then his father held up the newspaper. "You are actually giving her PR help?"

"She refused my bodyguard services. I'm pretty sure you were here when that happened."

"Damn stubborn girl." Lincoln Brown rubbed the flat of his palm over his chest.

"She's not a girl. She's a woman. And she handled herself just fine."

"Handled?" The judge's gaze narrowed. He should've known the lawyer would pick up on his word choice. "As in, something happened?"

"She was attacked." Marsh didn't pull his punches because these men needed to understand something was going on, and he couldn't protect her if he didn't know what it was. And she had been less than forthcoming.

"Where? When? How?" Lincoln Brown bulleted questions, his voice rising.

"In her condo, two nights ago, and allegedly he was just supposed to scare her."

"You saved her?" The judge raised a brow, a smile on his face.

"She saved herself." Much as it chafed. "But I need to know who you think is behind this."

The judge glanced at Lincoln Brown. "It would be better if you didn't know."

If he didn't know? What kind of response was that?

"I need a name."

"Is she okay?" Lincoln's voice graveled out.

Marsh didn't want to answer. "She's fine." That covered quite a bit of territory.

"Fine isn't an answer."

"She was rattled."

"Dammit," Lincoln muttered under his breath. He rubbed his hand over his chest, his eyes dark and wide with fear. "How do you know what he was supposed to do?"

"I tracked him down and asked him some questions and put the fear of God into him." Marsh was starting to get annoyed. He needed answers. "Now will you tell me what's going on?"

"I can't."

Fuck. What the hell was he going to do with the Brown family? They were the most tight-lipped clients he'd ever worked with. And he'd worked with known mafia guys willing to roll over on their bosses.

He shifted tactics. "Why did you take guardianship of Ayesha when she was thirteen?"

"Not my story to tell," Lincoln Brown said. Which seemed odd, considering. This family was one big secret. And it was annoying as hell.

Lincoln Brown rubbed his chest again.

"Are you okay?" Had Brown's face turned slightly gray?

Lincoln gasped. "I don't think so."

And then he collapsed.

Chapter 10

The hospital doors swished open and Ayesha ran through them. She'd gotten the call twenty minutes ago and had hopped in a Lyft immediately.

She must've looked frantic because the greeter at the door asked her, "Where do you need to go?"

"Cardiac floor."

"Four."

Ayesha waved her thanks and rushed toward the elevator. Her heart was going a million miles a minute. Not her Gramps too. She couldn't bear it. She was sweating and shaking and crumbling with fear inside. A cardiac event was what they'd said. He hadn't had heart problems a day in his life.

She rushed to the charge desk and asked, "Lincoln Brown?"

Before the nurse could tell her, Marsh Adams approached from her left. "This way."

"What are you doing here?" Her brain couldn't seem to make the leap.

"I was with your grandfather." Marsh grabbed her arm

gently and led her toward a room. "Luckily we got him here quickly."

"We?"

"Yeah. We were at the judge's office."

Ayesha said, "I need to see him."

"You didn't tell him you were attacked."

"You told him?" She was pissed. All her stress and worry over the past half hour finally had a target. "What the hell? It was none of your damn business." She stopped still, her fists clenched. This asshole was the reason her Gramps had a heart attack? "It was not your place."

"He needed to be told. And I need information about the threat."

"First of all, I didn't ask for or want a bodyguard. Second of all, I'll say it again. It's none of your damn business. And I didn't want to worry him." And, apparently, for good reason. Shit.

"I'm not going to apologize."

"Is he going to be okay?"

"They think so. But they're keeping him here today to monitor everything."

Relief swept through her like a tsunami and she sagged against him. She couldn't afford to be angry right now. She didn't want her Gramps to worry about anything. His job was to get better.

Marsh was practically holding her up. She didn't have the energy to push him away. If anything, she wanted his arms around her. Someone there to hold her up. To keep her company. And right now Marsh was her option.

"What happened?"

"They aren't exactly sure, but he has elevated levels of tro…troponin. He had palpitations and chest pain so they thought he might be having a heart attack. But the elevated levels can apparently just be brought on by stress without an actual event."

She rushed into the room and stopped at the sight of her grandfather lying in the hospital bed. He was hooked up to multiple monitors with leads on his chest, looking older than his seventy-odd years. "Gramps."

He opened his eyes and smiled tremulously. "Hey, girl."

She hustled to his side and grasped the hand that didn't have the pulse and oxygen monitor on it.

His grip was light and his smile shaky.

"You're okay." She patted him as if she could make it true.

"I will be." Always positive, her Gramps. He had been her savior when she was young and her rock since she'd become an adult. "What are you doing here?"

"Well, that's a dumb question." She held his hand clasped between hers and squeezed. "I'm here for you."

"Don't you need to be getting those paintings done?" Gramps said to Marsh, "I'm a decent artist but never even come close to Ayesha."

Her heart melted. "You taught me everything I know."

He looked at Marsh and smiled again. "My girl's an amazing painter. Always has been since she was a kid. Pure genius."

"Hush now."

Marsh stayed silent but nodded. Ayesha barely spared him a glance. Of course, she'd be asking him more questions once they were alone, but right now her focus was on her Gramps.

"A heart attack. You just trying to get some attention?"

"That's me," he huffed out a wheezy laugh. "Attention ho."

Ayesha forced a laugh out because her Gramps was the

furthest thing from an attention seeker. That had been her, until it all changed when she was thirteen.

"I'm sorry," he said. His expression was somber and his eyes full of regret.

"For scaring the heck out of me? You should be."

"Let me say my piece." He looked deep into her eyes, his whites rheumy and riddled with bloodshot, that deep fathomless brown that had always regarded her with love and acceptance. "Forgive me."

Emotion welled in her tight throat and her eyes watered. She had mostly come to terms with what had happened years ago. But there'd always been that kernel deep inside that mourned their old relationship. Because once she had done what he asked, her innocence had been gone forever. Trust with her was hard-fought and difficult to come by. But once she accepted, she loved freely and with her whole heart.

"I love you, Gramps."

"Love you too girl. Doesn't mean what I did was right."

She blinked back tears. "It's not important."

"But it is." He brushed her tears away and pulled her toward him. He pressed a kiss to her forehead and whispered, "Forgive me. I don't want to die with that on my conscience."

"You're not going to die," she shot back in horror.

"Well, hopefully not yet." His voice was stronger. "But if I'm going to go to my Maker, I want to go with an open heart and a clean conscience."

What the hell was he saying?

"Your conscience is just fine, Gramps. I forgive you." In that moment, she would say anything to get him to stop talking about death.

"I mean it, girl."

"I know you do. So do I." She leaned down and squeezed him tight, careful not to dislodge any of the multitude of wires and equipment hooked up to him. "No dying. You are forgiven."

"Just like that?"

"Absolutely. I love you." And she did. He had given her stability and love and acceptance when she needed it most. "Always. I'd do anything for you." And she had.

"I'm going to be fine. It's all going to be fine. Now get on home and finish up your masterpieces."

"I want to stay with you."

"No need." He smiled. "I'm tired. The doc said I should rest. No need for you to stay here and watch daytime TV. Get on home and finish up those paintings."

Her Gramps was as stubborn as she was. Sitting around here wasn't going to get things done. But she finally realized that if she didn't take care of his problem, her grandfather was going to let everything come out. She wasn't about to let him do that.

MARSH WAS FOLLOWING Ayesha at a discreet distance. After she had left the hospital room, he had promised her grandfather that he'd look out for her, so here he was acting like a creeper again.

Her weariness hung on her shoulders like a cape. She wasn't going home to finish her paintings and he wondered where she was headed. As he followed, she got closer and closer to the Mall downtown.

Marsh had questions. So many questions.

He followed her into the National Gallery of Art. Her

steps were deliberate. She knew exactly where she
was going.

She headed up the grand stairway and through the
doors, not stopping to admire the calm courtyard with its
bubbling fountain and plants and sunlight streaming
through the domed ceiling.

Marsh kept his distance…until she stopped, turned
around, and gave him a look with narrowed eyes and a
suspicious squint. In Ayesha language that was tantamount
to an invitation to join her. Marsh walked up carefully and
just stood next to her quietly.

She was studying a portrait. Something he would call
traditional, with dark, muted colors and soft lighting.

It was nothing like what she painted, and he wondered
what she saw in it.

"For a while, I tried to imitate other artists, but I finally
realized I just had to be me."

There was something there in her voice. He needed to
take note. This tepid portrait was nothing like her work. Her
painting was brilliant. Edgy. Dark. With a female mystique
missing from this.

"I'd say that you found your sweet spot."

She turned to look at him. "You don't like this?"

Marsh shrugged. "It's fine. But I like art that evokes
some sort of emotion and this…doesn't."

"Fine? This is a self-portrait, the ultimate Renaissance
selfie," she said. "By Rembrandt."

"Okay?"

"Rembrandt is considered one of the greatest masters of
all time. His paintings are the most stolen in history."

"If I was going to steal a painting, I'd steal yours."

A particular pleasure lit her hazel eyes and she nearly
glowed before some memory clearly shut it down.

She turned to stare at the Rembrandt again.

"What are we doing here?"

She moved on to the next picture, a landscape, another tepid painting, in his opinion. "This is my happy place."

"This art gallery? Or art museums in general?" He had a burning desire to know everything about her. It was a bad sign. He knew she and her grandfather were keeping things from him. He hated liars. And yet, he couldn't imagine that she had done anything awful. She was too bold, too out there, too in your face.

"Art museums." She tilted her head and looked at the painting. "I like to try to imagine where the artists were, what were they thinking…how did they feel about their art, their life, when they painted the specific painting?"

He had to confess he never looked at art that way before. "I always figured it was their job."

"Not for artists. Paintings have too much of the artists in them. And do we really know ourselves?"

"When you're looking at a painting that you created are you remembering how you felt?" Now he was thinking about the couple on that canvas in her condo.

"Every single one."

"Are there really that many?"

"I've been painting since I was eight."

Eight? That seemed a little young.

"Yes, it was young."

He hadn't said that aloud, had he?

"I can see your face. The question was written all over it."

"And when did you realize that you just had to be you?"

Ayesha pushed onto the next painting, this one by a different artist. "I was thirteen."

Thirteen? That age seems to be coming up quite a bit. "That's when your grandparents took guardianship of you?"

She stiffened. "I see someone's been doing their homework."

"I started investigating you as soon as my father asked me to be your bodyguard."

"Your father? I think that's the first time you've referred to him as your father and not the judge. What changed?"

Marsh shifted uncomfortably. Because several things his father had said to him in the office had hit home. That and Lincoln Brown's sincere request that Ayesha forgive him had swirled around in his brain. How could he ever expect forgiveness if he wasn't willing to forgive others? Which meant that he was going to have to figure out how to forgive his father.

"What did your grandfather want you to forgive?"

"None of your business."

"Well, it kind of is if it has anything to do with your attacker."

"You don't want to know." She pressed her lips together and he was reminded again of their kiss, of those moments on the sofa when he'd stared into her eyes and felt so connected to her, like nothing he'd ever felt with another person.

Maybe he didn't want to know.

"You're investigating me."

"I'm sure I can find out why your grandparents took over your care, but it would be easier if you just told me."

She shrugged. "Well, it turns out that when you're miserable in your own skin and you constantly act out that it creates friction in the house. Which then in turn makes everyone miserable."

Marsh had been too busy taking care of his mother to

act out, but it was pretty common. "Don't most teenagers act out?"

"Sure. But I was the opposite of everything my mother wanted. I'm an introvert. I just wanted to be alone. Instead I was constantly expected to be charming and entertaining at parties. And I hated it."

"What did you do?"

"You name it, I did it." Ayesha rubbed her palms over her biceps. "That pretty much sealed my mother's dislike of me. She didn't want the embarrassment of a rebel daughter."

"So how did you end up with your grandparents?"

"My mother didn't know how to deal with me. And my father went along with whatever she wanted." Ayesha walked to the next painting. "One day during a particularly…difficult argument, she yelled, 'if you love spending time with your Gramps so much, why don't you go live with him.'"

Ayesha rubbed her palms over her biceps and walked towards the exit. "And I so asked them, and Gramps and Gram agreed to take me. My parents bought their way into a foreign posting and there you have it."

"When was last time you saw her?"

She studied the ceiling contemplatively. "Four years ago?"

Four years. Wow.

"Right?" Her smile was quick and mischievous. "But it didn't matter because I had my grandparents."

"Your grandmother passed away….?"

"Last year." Her face saddened. "Only my dad came home for that."

"You aren't mad at your dad too?" Because her father hadn't stuck up for her.

"I'm not mad at either of them anymore." Ayesha said, "But it was a long slow road. And I was much happier with my grandparents. So it was win-win."

Her grandparents. What had her grandfather been talking about? "What was it that you needed to forgive?"

"I'm done with this interrogation."

That wasn't really fair.

"I've got things to do. See you later." She walked to another room.

Marsh followed. He knew she was hiding things from him. "I can help you."

"Maybe you can. But that's not how I roll."

She was determined to do this all by herself. He should just let her. He was supposed to be fixing his relationship with Jill and Kita and the rest of the Adams-Larsen employees, not chasing after some woman who didn't want his help. Except that she was an artist and she was in trouble. She didn't have resources that he did.

And he had promised his father.

He wasn't to get anywhere unless he opened up to her. "When I was twelve I walked in on my father having sex with an intern."

She stopped in her tracks. Turned. Her eyes were wide, surprised. "Wow."

"Yeah, not the sex education that the schools suggest."

"And you're telling me this…why?"

"My mom fell apart. She was an absolute mess going through the divorce. That was the first time I was compelled to protect someone. A woman."

She looked fascinated and he knew he had to keep talking. Otherwise, she'd walk away. He gestured to the bench in the center of the room. She sat and waited.

"When I was seventeen, my best friend, Kita, had an

issue with her mother, and we ended up taking her in. I jumped in right away to be her protector."

"Were you…?"

"No. Just friends." He thought about Kita now. They never even contemplated a romantic relationship.

"I see a pattern."

"You could say that. A few years ago, another friend, Jillian, had a problem when we worked for the US Marshals. We left together and started Adams-Larsen."

"The PR agency?" She said dubiously.

"Everyone assumed that I was rescuing her. But the truth was I wasn't happy at the Marshals. But now it's gotten to be a thing."

"And were you involved with *her*?"

"Nope. Just friends." He and Jill had considered a romantic relationship, but that was frowned on by the US Marshals' office and they weren't all that into each other.

"Any others?"

"Recently I tried to rescue a client. Except, it turned out she was using me."

Ayesha looked sick to her stomach. She pressed a hand to her belly. "What happened?"

"I let down everyone I care about. I'm trying to make amends."

"And you're telling me all this why?"

"All those people, I was rescuing them."

"I thought that we determined I don't want to be rescued."

"No, yeah, I get that. I don't want to rescue you."

Her face blanked. "Well then, great, we're on the same page." She jumped to her feet and looked ready to bolt.

Marsh stood quickly and clasped her by the biceps. He looked down into her eyes and said, "You don't understand.

I don't want to save you. I don't want to rescue you. But I would like to help you. I'd like to be your partner."

For a moment, Marsh thought he'd gotten through to her. Maybe, just maybe they could work together. But then she said, "Thanks for the offer. But no thanks."

Chapter 11

The next morning, Marsh's offer still rattled around in her brain and she wished, rather desperately, that she could take him up on it. Partners. It was disturbing how much that word tempted her. But the truth was she couldn't trust anyone. She had to do this alone.

She shrugged it off because what did it matter? She didn't have help. And even if she did want to trust Marsh, she couldn't.

She was angry. And she needed to funnel that anger into results.

She'd put on leggings and a sweater in soft cashmere. Tactile, sensuous, it soothed her as she headed out on her errands.

She first noted the guy following her while she was getting a hot tea at the coffee shop down the street from her loft. He had an interesting face. Slavic, maybe Russian features, blunt nose and sharp cheekbones, but with eyes that turned his face slightly pretty. He was in good shape, all sleek lines and muscled perfection. His hair was combed just so. And while his leather jacket had seen better days, it was clearly well taken care of. The thing was he never looked at her. Which would've been fine, except that he checked out every single other person in the café while she waited for her tea. And the fact that he didn't look at her put her senses on high alert. But then she'd left the café and he hadn't followed her so she assumed she'd been a little paranoid. And who could blame her?

Next stop was the library.

She needed to do some research on RFID tags. Putting a radio frequency tag on the frame of expensive paintings in museums was becoming more common. Jonathon Harrington the Third had had had radio frequency identification on the paintings displayed throughout his house. Chances were strong that his son, the Fourth, also had tags on the real Rembrandts, even though there was no way he could display the originals in the common areas of his house.

If she thought about the overall problem, she'd be paralyzed. Because she was an artist not a thief. So she broke it down into segments.

One. She needed to steal the originals from Harrington. She had to figure out when that asshole Harrington wouldn't be at home. He was too cheap to employ guards, but she would bet he had some form of electronic surveillance in place. She also knew he had a house alarm on his estate windows and doors.

Two. She needed to find a way to remove the fakes from the elder Harrington's house in Cape Cod without suspicion.

Three. This was without a doubt not a one-person endeavor. And yet she was going to have to do it alone. Then she had to substitute the originals while the fakes were out of the estate's possession.

She sat in a carrel in the library doing her internet searches. She had also Google Earth-ed Harrington's house in Virginia and searched online for architectural plans. Chances were he had the paintings in the secret room in his house. She was going to have to ask Gramps. But if she was wrong and there was a vault, she was screwed.

In which case she should probably be at home working on her last two submissions for the show so she'd have money. But for her Gramps, she had to try.

A few hours later, her eyes bleary from staring at the screen and reading about RFID and blueprints and thinking about how she could get all the moving parts to line up for the outcome she needed, she was ready to leave. As she paused at the exit to the library, she was pretty sure she caught a glimpse of the guy from the coffee shop again. Her heartbeat quickened. Fuck. He was smoother than the guy who'd broken into her apartment building, but what if he had also been hired to scare her. Or worse.

Maybe she was just being paranoid. After all, both the café and the library were in her neighborhood. Maybe he just happened to be near the same places as her. It happened. But she was determined to keep an eye on her surroundings.

Next stop was her parkour course. She didn't think she'd have to do any *Mission Impossible*-type shit, but agility was definitely something she needed to keep up with. And she needed to be ready for anything. Part of her couldn't even acknowledge that she was contemplating committing a crime and stealing the original paintings. The other part of her just wanted this to be over and her Gramps to be safe.

Ayesha went through the parkour course four times, picking up her speed every time. She only stumbled when it occurred to her that if she lost her balance, she could hurt her wrists and hands. She couldn't paint if she were injured.

She called a taxi and waited in the warm vestibule, digging through her hobo bag, making sure she had enough cash so that she didn't leave any kind of credit card trail. Thanks to an obsession with Criminal Minds when she was younger, she knew to avoid electronic payments. In a few minutes, the taxicab pulled up to the curb. She glanced around once again looking for the blond-haired man, but she didn't see him anywhere. She subtly relaxed and jogged to the taxi. She slid in and requested the local sporting goods store.

Ten minutes later, she was roaming the store, searching for the things she might potentially need to pull this off. Although how she was going to make it happen, she still hadn't quite figured out. But she would.

After picking up gloves, rope, hat, and other climbing paraphernalia, she paid for her belongings and once again waited for a taxi.

A flash of brown leather caught her eye and she turned her head. He was there again. He stared at her for a moment, then mouthed, "Fuck."

With a determined stride he headed toward her.

For a moment decision paralysis kept her in place. Stay in the store where there were lots of people around? Or run?

She didn't know. But if she called attention to herself and anything happened, there could potentially be a record of her purchases here and she could not afford for that to happen.

Decision made, she rushed out the door.

A light snow had started to fall, and the sidewalks were

slick. She didn't run. She didn't want to call attention to herself, but she walked quickly.

"Hold up," the man called with a bit of an accent.

Not a chance in hell.

Ayesha walked faster, heading toward the bus stop. She could see the bus rumbling along in the distance. If she could just hop on before the guy got there, she would be safe. Didn't matter what bus it was or where it was going as long as she got away from him.

"I am not here to hurt you," he called out again.

Not falling for that. Ayesha rushed up to the bus stop just as the doors hissed open and the pneumatic step dropped. She hustled on and dropped money in the receptacle. Then she headed to the back of the bus and ducked down into the corner.

The guy wasn't going to make it. She could see him flat-out running now, but the bus doors closed and it began to rumble along the street. He caught up and banged the side with the palm of his hand. Her gaze caught his and he swore again. Then he mouthed something she couldn't quite understand and pulled out his phone.

A few seconds later, her phone began to ring. Her heart was beating a million miles a second as adrenaline rushed through her body. Marsh was calling her.

"What?" she barked into the phone.

"I'm sorry." Before she could say anything else— Because why would he be sorry?—he said, "That was my guy, Viktor."

His *guy*? "Are you serious?"

"I didn't want you to be unprotected. So I had him follow you." Marsh was silent for a second. Ayesha was so pissed she couldn't speak. "I can't believe you saw him."

"Well, it wasn't that freaking hard. He was following me." Steam began to build. "You scared the shit out of me."

His voice softened. "I'm sorry. I just didn't think it was a good idea for you to be alone."

"Well, perhaps you could have given me a heads-up."

"Would you have accepted my help?"

He had her there. But as other things sank in, she realized Marsh's guy had been following her all morning. So now someone had a record of where she'd been and what she'd done. She thunked her head on the bar on the seat in front of her and swore softly.

"I can help you."

"Let go of that savior complex." Even though the temptation to lean on him was there. Because her thoughts kept going back to worrying about how she was going to get this all done. It wasn't a one-person job.

"I'm trying, but in the meantime, you're stuck."

Oddly, she appreciated his honesty. And it wasn't a one-person job. While she had been running through the parkour course, her brain had worried over details. "Maybe I'll let you."

"Wait. What?"

"I'm conceding that perhaps I need some help."

"Well great, while I've got you on the phone, can you come into the office so we can discuss your PR plan?"

"I thought we had already done that."

"We have some other things to run by you and a more comprehensive plan. I think I can get a feature in the art section of the paper. But we need to move quickly."

A feature in the paper. That would be phenomenal. "Can we highlight the other artists?"

"We can highlight you. And you can mention the other artists."

This was why she didn't like publicity. She was a private person. Basically she just wanted to paint her paintings and live her life. But everything had gotten so complicated.

"And then we can talk about your security."

Ugh.

VIKTOR WALKED into Marsh's office. He closed the door quietly and sat in the chair across from Marsh's desk.

"What the hell happened?"

Viktor sighed heavily. Marsh noticed the lines of strain around his eyes. "She made me."

"That's not like you." And it wasn't. Viktor was dedicated, intense. He was hypervigilant in his work, as if he were always trying to make up for the fact that he wasn't born in this country. "Jill said you were instrumental in finding Brianna."

"Yeah, too bad I fucked it all up by sleeping with Malachi."

So that's what this was about. "Let it go, man." Marsh jolted. Perhaps he needed to take his own advice.

"I will make it up to you," Viktor vowed.

Marsh focused on his more immediate issue. "She saw you?"

"First thing. She made me in the coffee shop."

Marsh considered that.

Interesting. Because the other day when he followed her, she'd been completely oblivious. "How did she seem?"

"Nervous. Paranoid."

Shit. And he had made that worse by having Viktor look out for her. "Okay. Give me a sit rep. Where did she go? What did she do?"

Viktor detailed Ayesha's morning. Library computer system. That was interesting.

"She has a laptop in her condo, why would she go to the library?"

"Internet searches she didn't want anyone to know about."

Interesting. "I wish I knew what she'd been looking up."

"Oh ye of little faith." Viktor pulled up something on his phone. "She spent quite a bit of time on RFIDs."

Radio Frequency Identification?

"She also checked out an estate of a Virginia address. She spent quite a bit of time studying Google Earth images of the house and land."

He didn't like where his brain was going.

"How did you find that out?"

"Do you really want to know?"

"Okay, fancy cloning or whatever. I should probably tell you that was an invasion of her privacy, however, thank you." See, he could deal with shades of gray.

Viktor nodded and then continued.

"Parkour again." Marsh repeated.

"Yeah. And she was good."

Parkour you could explain away. She had excess energy and wanted to release it.

"Sporting goods store?"

Viktor nodded.

"What did she buy?"

"All things that could be used to conceal features if you were doing something where you didn't want to be noticed. And some ropes and climbing equipment."

What the hell was she up to?

Before Marsh could say anything else, the intercom on his desk phone rang. "There's an Ayesha Brown to see you."

"Great. I'll be right there." Marsh stood quickly. It had only been a few hours and he was still anxious to see her, anxious to touch her. "Thanks for your help, Viktor." Viktor nodded, but Marsh could tell something was still on his mind. "Is everything okay?"

"It will be. Just working through some stuff."

"You can always talk to me, you know."

"I know."

Marsh headed for the reception area where the new girl sat.

Ayesha stood in the small room, curiously glancing around. She turned when she heard him coming and her attitude morphed. Her chin went up, her eyes narrowed, and she said, "Okay. I'm willing to let you help me."

Marsh's heart took an instant leap. But he had to wonder. "What changed?"

"Not here."

"Come on in." Marsh ushered her into Jillian's office. Because he had made the commitment to keep his partner apprised of everything and he wasn't about to fuck up the best relationship he'd ever had. Especially over a woman who was keeping secrets. Lots of secrets.

Marsh introduced them. "I'd like you to meet my partner, Jill." Jill stood up and smooth her palms down her perfect straight skirt. "Jill, this is Ayesha Brown."

Jill put on that smile she saved for annoying people. Most of the time she used it when his father was around. She came around her desk and held out her hand. The two women shook quickly and then dropped hands as if burned. "What can we do for you?"

Ayesha glanced between the two of them. "Public relations?"

"Of course." Jill gestured towards the seating arrangement in the middle of the room. "Have a seat."

Ayesha perched on the edge of the love seat.

"Just give me a minute to pull up the more comprehensive plan we put together."

Marsh compared the two women. Jill with her ice-blonde hair smoothed into a tight bun, retro suit with a pencil skirt and fitted jacket, and calm, unemotional features. Ayesha with her wildly curling hair, loose sweater and leggings, and every emotion flitting across her face. They couldn't be more opposite in appearance but both of them had an inner core of strength that amazed him. He realized how much he wanted them to get along. But based on Jill's closed-off face and Ayesha's defiant one that was probably going to take some time.

Marsh had the feeling that Ayesha wanted to say something, but she kept her lips tightly sealed and crossed her arms. He recognized the defensive posture immediately.

Jill sat in the wing chair across from the love seat and placed the folder on the coffee table. "Would you like something to drink?"

"Nope."

Jill ticked through the items that their PR branch had put together. "The objective is to get eyes on the show, whether the target attends or not. While opening night is important, you want all those people coming into the gallery after the holidays to spend their gift money. The strategy is to do a quick blast."

Ayesha studied the file.

"Your audience is older with more disposable income although young up-and-coming politicians and staffers might have dollars to spend if they're from wealthier families."

"True."

"We don't necessarily have time for research and insights into the data so we're going to have to use tried-and-true channels to get the word out."

Ayesha said, "Didn't we pretty much cover this the other day?"

Jill raised a brow. "We do also want you to use more social media."

Ayesha shuddered.

"Facebook is the place for your main demographic, however Instagram is so visual it would be a good medium as well. We've created a business profile for you. You can keep it all about your process and inspiration. It doesn't need to be pictures of you. I'm assuming that you are proficient with a camera phone." Jill's voice was brisk and businesslike. "We also need a press kit. Do you have a headshot or do we need to schedule one?"

Ayesha looked like her head was spinning. "You don't screw around."

"And a biography. We'll send notifications to all traditional print outlets and online newspapers and any other places that the gallery owner wishes."

"I'll ask her," Ayesha said faintly. "She was excited about the exposure."

It looked pretty good as far as he could tell. Ayesha made a couple of minor comments. "One thing. I want the names of the other artists in everything sent out."

A new respect entered Jill's gaze and she nodded, making notes on the paper. "I'll make sure that happens."

Marsh had stayed silent, beginning to relax as the atmosphere had loosened a little bit in the last few minutes.

"Now that were done with that," Ayesha said. "Why the hell did you have someone following me?"

"If you aren't doing anything wrong, then it shouldn't matter," Jill shot back.

"And there it is." Ayesha frowned at Jill.

"I'm just saying."

"What I do is none of your business."

"It is if Marsh thinks you need protection."

Now he was in the middle of it. Great. "Let's everybody take a breath."

Both women whipped their heads towards him. "Fuck you," they said in stereo.

Marsh blinked.

"Asking for help was a mistake." Ayesha gathered her stuff and was getting ready to leave.

"Wait a minute. You didn't ask for help," Marsh said desperately.

"Good thing."

"What do you need help with?"

"Nothing a *PR company* can help me with." She sneered the words.

"Now we're getting to it," Jill said.

Marsh tried to defuse the situation between the two of them. "What do you need help with?" He couldn't help the leap in his heart. Because maybe he had finally gotten through to her this morning.

"My grandfather has an important appraisal coming up and we need security for it."

"Security?" Jill raised an eyebrow.

"Well, if you read the papers, that is something Adams-Larsen is into."

"You believe everything you read the paper?"

Shit. They were starting to get aggressive again.

"What kind of security?" Marsh drew their focus to him.

"We need to pick up two paintings. Rembrandts." She

shot a glance at Marsh. "And get them secured in a vault until my grandfather can appraise them."

"How is your grandfather?" Jill's voice had softened.

Ayesha's gaze turned pensive. "A little better. He is getting released from the hospital after his stress test if all goes well. But he needs to take it easy."

"We might be able to help with that," Jill said. "Where? And when?"

"I have to get the exact details, but the house is on Cape Cod."

Marsh couldn't help but be thankful it wasn't in Virginia. But then what was she doing looking up specs for a house in Virginia?

"Doesn't your grandfather have his own security?"

"Normally, yes, he oversees everything himself. But I don't want him to have to go all the way to Massachusetts to do this. I said I would handle it."

"And where is the vault?"

"In DC."

"When does need to be done?"

"December 23rd."

"That's…an interesting time of the year."

"The estate wants it done before December 31st, and my Gramps wants to get it out of the way so the paintings can be delivered to the museum before the end of the fiscal year."

"What's the rush?"

"Tax issues."

"What's the name and address of the estate?" Jill scratched something on the paper at her desk. Jillian was suspicious. "And why choose us?"

Marsh also had to wonder why the 23rd. That was the date of Ayesha's show. The timing was…odd.

SO THIS WAS THE PARTNER. Ayesha studied Jillian Larsen.

The one Marsh blew up his career for. And if they were a PR firm, she was a comic book artist. She couldn't help but admire the fact that Jillian Larsen wasn't looking at the surface. Even though they'd started off on the wrong foot. Sort of.

"My Gramps wants you to do it."

"And why would your Gramps think that we could?" Jill asked quickly before Marsh could get a word in.

"Because Judge Adams indicated that you were trustworthy."

At that Marsh bristled.

"Of course we are," Jill replied.

"Don't get your panties in a twist." Ayesha smirked. She wasn't crazy about using them. But it could kill two birds with one stone.

Marsh interrupted. "December 23rd is the day of your show."

He remembered? "Yeah. The timing isn't optimal." *Actually…a lie.*

This way, Harrington couldn't accuse Gramps, or Ayesha, of stealing the fakes since they would be at her show in DC and not on the Cape in Massachusetts. They would have an ironclad alibi. It was minor but it covered them just in case there were questions later, or Harrington lost his mind and somehow accused Gramps of stealing something.

She wished that she could stick it to Harrington. Implicate him in some way. But the only way to do that was to put her grandfather in peril. And she refused to do that.

"We don't typically handle merchandise," Jillian said.

Which made her wonder what it was they did usually handle.

"Well, if you can't do it—"

"No one said we couldn't do it."

Marsh was studying her, and she didn't like it. He knew more about her relationship with her grandfather than she would like. "This just came up?" Marsh asked.

"Yes." Ayesha forced her face to be expressionless. "My Gramps got the call this morning." Even though he'd known it was likely coming.

"Seems very last minute."

Ayesha shrugged. "People with money do things last minute all the damn time. We're lucky they didn't decide they needed to have it done Christmas day after dinner was over."

Jillian chuckled. "True."

"You'll need to get insurance," Ayesha said. "My Gramps has coverage once the paintings are in his vault, but as the transport company, you should as well."

Jillian scratched another note on the paper. "How much?"

"I'm not exactly sure. But I would guess about twenty million."

Jillian didn't show any outward sign of surprise, however the pen was digging into the paper.

Ayesha's stomach twisted. Holy shit. Twenty million dollars. If she couldn't pull this off, she was going to prison. For a very long time. Sweat broke out on her brow.

"Twenty. Million?" Marsh interrupted their back and forth. There was a look on his face that she couldn't interpret.

"Yeah. That's why they want it done before the end of the year. The elder Harrington passed away and he wanted to donate the paintings to a small museum in DC. Much to the dismay of his son."

Jillian snorted.

Ayesha looked at her with new eyes. "You know him?"

"We're acquainted." Jillian tapped her pen on the notebook she was holding. "I bet Harrington the Fourth was pissed when he found out his father donated them to a museum."

"You could say that." Ayesha couldn't wait to screw him. Entitled jerk.

"What's our risk?" Jillian asked again.

"Should be minimal, unless someone tries to steal the things in transit."

"If we can take care of people with sentience and free will and who can make jobs difficult…"

Ayesha stifled a laugh.

"…then we should be able to handle two inanimate objects."

"There will be chain-of-custody paperwork that has to be completed. But the paintings should also have RFID tracking devices on the frames."

Marsh jolted. He'd been letting her and Jillian hash out the details, but something was bothering him. And it freaked her out a little bit that she could tell that something was bothering him.

He asked, "Is that common?"

"More and more so. It's become easy technology to deploy. I mean hey, the bras I buy have tags sewn into their lining."

"What bras?" he blurted out and then flushed.

Oops. True. It was her turn to flush.

"The paintings will need to be crated, then go straight from the estate to the secure vault at my grandfather's office.

And then my grandfather will appraise them from December 26th through the 30th. Then they will be transported to the museum on the 31st."

"Do you need us to do the second transport?" Jillian asked.

"Because it's all within fifty miles, I believe the second leg can be done by Gramps's regular company. But I will check with him."

"And where is your grandfather now?" Jillian asked.

"I'm about to go pick him up from the hospital."

"Excellent. I'll take care of getting the logistics settled on this." Jill shot Marsh a look. "Your grandfather can communicate any other specifics we need to know regarding the transport of priceless paintings so we can nail down the details."

"Sounds good."

"Marsh, you go with her to help get Lincoln Brown home."

She needed to talk to her Gramps—alone. Let him know that she had this under control and she would take care of everything. Take care of *him*. "That's not necessary."

"Oh, I insist."

"Happy to. I'll drive." Marsh foiled her attempt to get out of the office without an escort. He curled his hand around her biceps as they headed toward the Adams-Larsen parking lot. "How were you going to get him home? You don't have a car."

"I would've figured it out."

"Isn't it great? Now you don't have to," he said cheerfully.

"Great," she replied faintly. She was well and truly stuck.

Chapter 12

Marsh entered the hospital beside Ayesha.

She had tried to get him to stay in the car and wait. She didn't want him here, which immediately raised his suspicions. Why not?

She punched the button for the cardiac floor and they rode the elevator in silence. When the doors opened, she headed straight for the nurse's desk.

"Is there anything else we need to take care of before my grandfather is discharged?"

The nurse, in teal scrubs with black hearts sprinkled on them, smiled. "He is all set. He can go whenever he's ready. Although he's got a visitor right now."

Marsh was far enough away that he could see the small jerk in Ayesha's body.

"Who is visiting?" Her smile was tight, fake. The exact one she had given him the other night at dinner.

"I didn't catch his name."

Ayesha wasn't looking at the nurse, she was studying the sign-in sheet and if anything, her body language got tighter.

"Well, we'll just go in and say hi," she said gaily. Her

smile became more brittle, and he knew something
was wrong.

She turned to Marsh. "If you go get the car and drive
around to the front, I'll bring Gramps down in the
wheelchair and we can take off."

She didn't want him in her grandfather's hospital room.
It was the second time she'd tried to get rid of him. His
suspicion meter shot into the red zone. Who was visiting her
grandfather? And why didn't she want Marsh and the
mystery guest to meet?

"I'll come on in and see if there's anything I can take to
the car with me."

"That's not necessary," she said through gritted teeth.

"'Course it is." Marsh headed toward Lincoln's hospital
room. "You are going to have your hands full with the
wheelchair."

She pivoted and walked with a jerky, uneven gait.
Nothing like her normal loose-limbed saunter.

When they had almost reached her grandfather's room,
an older white dude exited. The heavy door eased closed
slowly. His face was set in as much of a frown as his Botox
would allow, but when he turned and saw them, his
expression changed in a blink. A smarmy smile coated his
mouth. "Well, look at that." The man held out his hand as
if to shake Ayesha's. "Ayesha Brown. I haven't seen you since
you were a young girl."

"How are you, Mr. Harrington?"

Harrington? None other than the man whose family was
donating the paintings. Marsh perked up.

"I was sorry to hear about your father," Ayesha said.

"Yes, our whole family is in mourning." Some emotion
darkened Harrington's blue eyes. "He was a hell of a man."

The words were all correct, but Marsh didn't get any

sense of grief from this guy. Of course, maybe he just hid it well. Everyone's response to grief was different.

"And who is this?"

"Just a friend helping me take my Gramps home."

Oh hell no. Marsh jammed out his hand and shook Harrington's, squeezing a little harder than he needed to. "Marsh Adams."

Ayesha tensed. Did she not want Harrington to know Marsh's firm was going to be transporting his father's paintings?

"Friend of the family." He avoided mentioning ALIAS and she subtly relaxed.

"Nice to meet you." Harrington shifted his gaze to Ayesha once more. "You take good care of your grandfather. Life can change in the blink of an eye."

Marsh's entire body quivered at the threat. Subtle but there.

Ayesha nodded shortly and pushed into her grandfather's hospital room.

Harrington walked away casually. What was the deal there? You could damn well bet that he was going to ask later.

Before Marsh followed Ayesha into the hospital room, he shot a quick text to Kita. *Check into the relationship between Lincoln Brown and the Harrington family, specifically the son.*

They already knew that the deceased father had been Lincoln Brown's mentor. Could the Fourth have been jealous of Lincoln's relationship with his father? Maybe that's what the exchange had been about. But then why visit Lincoln in the hospital?

Ten-four. Kita responded.

He followed Ayesha into the room where she and her grandfather were having a heated whispered discussion.

They both shut up when Marsh entered. Another thing he was going to have to ask about later.

"Hey, Mr. Brown. We're here to spring you." Marsh walked in as if he hadn't noticed their argument. And what was she doing arguing with the man? He just had a heart incident. "Have you got any stuff for me to take to the car?"

"Just me in the wheelchair." He sounded tired, and even worse, he looked defeated.

There had to be some connection between taking those paintings out of the house on Cape Cod and the fact that Harrington was here in Lincoln Brown's hospital room. Unless Harrington was just checking on the logistics. But again, why come to Lincoln's hospital room when a phone call would have sufficed?

"Okay, you guys take care of the paperwork and I'll bring the car around."

"What I wanted you to do five minutes ago," Ayesha snapped.

He was about to snark back at her, but he saw her worry and stress and he couldn't do it.

He knew she was lying to him. They both were. And yet his first emotion wasn't anger. It was concern. He wanted to help her, to smooth away those little lines of worry on her forehead and take away the shadows that darkened her eyes.

Completely the wrong reaction and yet he couldn't help himself.

Lincoln Brown glanced between the two of them. "Marsh is here to help?"

Ayesha smiled at her Gramps, the worry in her face disappearing smoothly into a real smile. "Yes, Gramps." She stroked her palm over the old man's shoulder. "Marsh is here to help."

Tension eased from the man's shoulders. "Good. That's good."

"I convinced his firm to do the removal of Mr. Harrington's paintings. You know, the ones you are going to appraise."

That was weird. She was talking to the old man as if he were an idiot.

"That way you don't have to worry about the security. They are moving them to the vault so you can appraise them right after Christmas."

The old man's gray eyebrows went up. His gaze shot to Marsh. "Thank you. When are you going to pick them up?"

Marsh paused. Shouldn't he know when the pictures were going to picked up?

"Gramps. I told you not to worry. I've got this."

He looked at Ayesha again. "You sure?"

"Yes, Gramps."

"And Marsh is helping you?"

"Yes, sir," Marsh concurred, but he wondered…what the hell was going on?

Unfortunately, he knew she wasn't about to share.

THE NEXT DAY, Ayesha was still on edge. She'd planned out what she could and she'd been actively finishing her paintings, even though she was worried sick about the next week. So many things could go wrong. And she didn't want to let down her Gramps. It was her turn to take care of him.

The doorbell rang. She glanced at the giant clock on the wall. Shit. She had lost track of time and she wasn't ready.

She shrugged. *Fuck it.* This article was about her paintings, and the show, not about her. She buzzed Marsh

and the reporter up and decided to make herself a cup
of tea.

A few minutes later, Marsh knocked on her front door.
Four knocks, three soft then one hard. It threw her that she
recognized his knock. She had literally met him less than a
week ago and already she knew some of his idiosyncrasies.

That unsettled her as well.

She opened the door. He looked delicious in jeans, a
button-down shirt with the collar open, and a casual navy
sport coat. He had loafers on his feet and his hair had been
combed. She peered at him. He looked like every prep-
school boy she'd ever encountered. Which was more than
her fair share, given her mother's background. "Do you
have gel in your hair?"

He blushed. "A little. It's long and I need a haircut." He
stepped inside and looked around her loft.

It was a mess. She waited for the explosion. Everyone
always wanted something from her. Always had
expectations. And if you knew you were going to live down
to those expectations, then why bother?

"Go get dressed."

She ignored him and peered over his shoulder. "Where's
the reporter?"

"I gave us half an hour to get your place ready."

"Seriously?" She cocked her head and gave him a death
stare.

He paused in his path to the kitchen and looked at her.
"You've been painting nonstop, haven't you?"

That took all the bravado out of her. "Yeah," she said.

"Okay. I'll get the rest of the place tidied up, if you go
put on some clothes that make you look like an up-and-
coming artist—" he scanned her quickly "—and not one
step up from homeless."

She started to argue with him. She might not be all primped-out and ready to be Instagrammed—she'd been posting on her official artist account as ordered—but she looked like she'd been painting.

As painters did.

Then she realized he was grinning.

"Gotcha." He waved his hand. "Put on whatever you're comfortable in. Don't worry about makeup. I'm pretty sure Allison is bringing a makeup person."

"A makeup person?"

"Sure. It'll take them a few minutes to set up as well. They'll have lights and umbrellas to reflect it and other stuff to create the right lighting for the pictures."

"Ugh." She guessed she would go change.

"How did it turn out?" Marsh headed toward the large painting in the corner.

She rushed past him and threw her body in front of the covered canvas, spreading her arms and legs so he couldn't get to it. "No."

He paused and narrowed his gaze. "Why not?"

"You can see it when everyone else does."

"But," he sputtered. "I have a vested interest in how it turned out."

"No." She didn't want him to judge the painting. The level of possessiveness she felt for the canvas was already off the charts. And if he hated it, she didn't want to know.

She had poured every ounce of sensuality and remembrance of their time together into the art.

"Fine. Go get dressed and I'll tidy up a little."

MARSH PEEKED at the painting while Ayesha was getting

ready. His heart beat a staccato tempo as he studied the painting of the two of them. It was…stunning.

He tried to look at the work objectively. The lines were sensual and evocative. But he couldn't quite disassociate himself from the feelings that the painting aroused. His cock stiffened as he remembered her riding him, her skin gleaming in the early morning light and her tits bouncing with every pump of his hips.

He inhaled sharply and let the covering drop. Jesus, he needed to get his body under control. As much as he'd teased her about the state of her condo, it was fairly clean. Her habit of cleaning her equipment after she was done painting clearly overflowed into other aspects of her life. Her cereal bowl and last night's dinner dishes were washed and resting in the dish drainer on the counter next to her giant farm sink. Even the quartz countertops had been wiped down and were clutter free.

He put away her dishes and prowled around the loft, picking up a sweater wrap thrown over the end of the sofa. He lifted the soft cotton to his nose and inhaled the unique scent of Ayesha's shampoo and linseed oil.

He tossed it in the hamper in the laundry area quickly, thankful no one saw him sniffing her clothing like a pervert.

Marsh glanced around for one last check. Other paintings were propped around the loft, mostly under the industrial metal windows that let in the light. And he could visualize the backdrop of the photos for the feature spread.

Ayesha exited her bedroom. In a few minutes she'd managed to transform from the messy paint-splattered imp into a sleek, sexy artist. She wore walnut brown leggings with a long, loose burnt-orange sweater that dipped off one shoulder, revealing bare soft skin that matched her leggings. Her hair was a loose blousy halo around her face, and she'd added shimmering color to her cheeks and eyelids and draped a trio of wood bangles on her wrists. But she'd left her feet bare as she stalked toward him.

As he studied her, his gaze heated, and her nipples tightened into sharp points. She paused a foot away. "Am I presentable enough in this outfit?"

"You're presentable in nothing." His voice was husky.

Her lids drooped and her breath soughed in a soft exhalation.

The doorbell rang as he was about to lower his head.

They broke apart. Shit. He needed to stop kissing her. Or almost kissing her. She was keeping things from him. Pretty large things he was sure, and he couldn't afford to ignore the warnings his intuition was throwing his way. That her secrets would have the power to harm him if he let himself be swayed by her.

Ayesha let the reporter in her loft.

"Hi, I'm Allison. This is Tony and Beth." She gestured to the cameraman with a suitcase full of equipment in tow and a thin woman with a case full of makeup.

Tony nodded at them. "Okay if I start setting up?"

"Go ahead," Allison said. "We'll just get started…" She glanced around. "Beth can get your makeup on and then we'll sit on the sofa."

"Sounds good."

Beth opened her case and got to work. Allison strode over to Marsh.

"You must be Marsh." Allison thrust out her hand and squeezed his. "Zara told me you'd be here."

Marsh smiled easily. "Nice to meet you."

They chit-chatted for a few moments while Beth worked.

"You're just here to assist the client, correct?"

"Yep. Pretend I'm not here." Marsh melted into the kitchen and sat at one of the stools at the breakfast bar.

Allison and Ayesha sat on the sofa. Marsh tried to forget what they'd done on that sofa. He knew Ayesha was having the same problem when she shot him a mischievous look.

Allison held up her smart phone. "Okay if I record our conversation?"

Ayesha nodded. "Just so we're up-front, I'm not very comfortable with this."

"Don't worry. This is a puff piece. My job is to get accurate information about the show and to make you look good so our readers will have events to attend. Nothing scary at all."

Allison put Ayesha at ease. She drew her out talking about the loft and the neighborhood. Then she asked, "What compelled you to start painting?"

"My grandfather gave me brushes and canvas when I was young. I studied the masters."

"Your painting is very abstract." Allison smiled and glanced at the paintings along the wall underneath the windows. "And you have a unique style. How did that come about?"

"I used to try and imitate other artists. But one day I had an epiphany and started developing my own style."

"What do you want people to think when they see your paintings?"

"I want art to be accessible. You should be your own gatekeeper. Figure out what you like and go for it. Don't let anyone else tell you what you should and shouldn't like."

"Who influenced you?"

"Aminah Robinson is my shero."

"Who is she?"

"She was an African-American artist who used

techniques learned from her father and mother as well as studying in art school. Her art was a mixture of all disciplines and techniques. She grew up in the projects in Columbus, Ohio. Her work was specific to the community she grew up in and yet universal."

Allison murmured indistinctly urging Ayesha to continue.

"She was very encouraging to young artists. My work holds no similarity to hers except for my level of immersion and intensity. But she inspired me to be true to my own roots, which are a melding of both my mother's and father's families and my education."

Allison said, "I'll have to check her out."

"She was awarded a MacArthur Fellowship, which was a huge honor. Her art was accessible and until very late in life affordable."

Allison said, "Your paintings are very expensive now."

"True. That's why this show isn't just about me. The entire exhibit is up-and-coming women artists of color." Ayesha passionately explained her driving force behind getting this show off the ground and giving other artists a platform. "Women in general have been overlooked as artists for centuries. I like to think that's changing."

Allison asked, "What makes your art special?"

"Art should make you feel something. It should touch you viscerally—on an intimate and personal level. My goal to is evoke emotion."

"Is there a theme for this show?"

"Shade: Discovering Color in a World of Darkness."

Allison's brow crimped for a moment and then understanding dawned. "I think that's great for the piece. Just a few pictures and then we'll get out of your hair."

She signaled to the photographer and he got to work.

Marsh watched Ayesha tense up when it was time to take the pictures, but Allison managed to put her at ease and the photo shoot went smoothly.

Allison stuffed her notebook and phone back in her messenger bag and came over to chat with him. "Thanks to Adams-Larsen for the lead and the introduction. I'll be in touch regarding the other article."

She smiled at him.

In order to get this shoved up the newspaper's production line, they'd had to promise a piece on ALIAS. Which made Marsh's skin crawl. Even though he and Jillian were discussing ways to make parts of ALIAS more transparent, a news article?

But the Browns were important to his father, and Marsh had an inconvenient fascination with Ayesha that didn't seem to be going away. Even if he wanted it to. They'd played on Allison's goals to move out of lifestyle pieces and into more newsworthy in-depth articles.

"Sounds good." He'd plan to be out of the office that day.

They packed up and left.

And it was just him and Ayesha again.

SHE HADN'T LIKED the way that the reporter looked at him. Which was stupid. The sense of possessiveness that had overcome her when the woman had put her hand on Marsh's arm was nuts.

"That went well."

As well as could be expected.

The awkwardness between them increased.

Ayesha prowled around her loft, unable to settle. She

needed to get these paintings to the gallery so that the owner could get them framed and hung before next week's show.

"I have a confession to make," Marsh said.

A confession? She blinked, wondering what he could possibly confess. She on the other hand, had plenty of things that she didn't want to be asked about, and if he knew half of them, he wouldn't be sitting at her kitchen island smiling.

"I don't want to know." She was just going to get it out there quickly.

He frowned. "What? Why not?"

"I'm not in the mood to share. I have things to do."

"Why do you have to be so contrary?"

Contrary? "If you don't like it, just leave."

Somehow their exchange had escalated. Marsh stalked toward her, a glint in his eye.

"I was going to compliment you. I am in awe of your talent." He loomed over her, a confused frown on his face. His brown eyes glimmered with some emotion she couldn't identify.

"That's very kind—"

"I'm not trying to be kind." Marsh gentled his voice. He skimmed his thumb over her bare shoulder. "I'm trying to tell you that your work evokes my emotions."

Exactly what she wanted. What she'd told the reporter.

"Oh," she sighed softly.

He traced his forefinger over the curve of her ear and down along her neck across her shoulder to the edge of her sweater.

She shivered at the sensual caress.

"Yeah, oh."

Had he leaned closer? Ayesha felt herself swaying

toward him. A bad, bad idea. But as she looked up into his face, she saw his simmering lust.

Without consent, she melted against him, gripping his waist through his jeans belt loop.

He hadn't taken his gaze from her as his hand slid down the bare skin of her chest until his palm hovered over her breast.

Ayesha inhaled, the move lifting her breast so it brushed his hand. *Touch me.*

"It makes me want…" Marsh bent closer still, trapping her with the heat in his gaze. "Want all sorts of things."

He traced his finger over the soft sweater, circling her nipple with his pointer finger. Ayesha's breath quickened. Her nipples tightened and warmth spread low in her belly.

"What sorts of things?" she breathed against his mouth, dying for him to kiss her. Dying for a harder touch of his hand. Dying for the erection prodding her belly.

The kiss was soft. He traced her lips with his tongue before slipping inside smoothly. He continued to play with her nipples, but his touch was too light.

"Harder."

He laughed against her lips. "No." His touch featherlight, he skimmed one hand beneath her sweater and smoothed his palm over the curve of her ass, trailing his fingers over the constricting leggings.

His mouth continued its lazy exploration of her lips, kissing her as if they had all the time in the world.

Turnabout was fair play. She tugged his button-down from the waist of his jeans and scraped her fingernails across his belly. His abs contracted and he nipped at her mouth.

Yes! Now he would push her against the wall and take this to the next level.

Instead he gentled his touch again and kissed a line from

the corner of her mouth to her earlobe. He slid his hand beneath her leggings, the tight material trapping his fingers against her bare skin. He continued sliding his hand down until his fingers touched her sex.

Ayesha moaned into his neck as he played with her clit, the touch so light it was there and then gone.

She sucked the skin where his neck met his collarbone, requesting without words a harder touch. Her fingers nimbly worked the buttons on his shirt and soon she had the bare expanse of his chest to play with.

Ayesha trailed her tongue over his muscles. His preppy boy clothes hid a spectacular body. She stopped to play with his nipples sucking then biting gently, hoping to prod him into moving faster.

Instead he slid his finger inside her, oh so gently and held there, his palm cupping her mound and his middle finger just so, while his other hand pressed her into the erotic touch.

Her knees weakened. "Marsh," she begged.

He chuckled. Actually laughed. And she might have gotten mad, except she needed him to move faster. To fill her up. To make her come.

"Not here." He smiled slowly, his mouth slick with their kisses.

"Anywhere," she said quickly, undoing his belt buckle.

He stopped her. The tip of his cock peeked out of his waistband.

"That has got to be painful."

"You can fix it for me in a second."

She quickly unzipped his pants and wrapped her hand around him, savoring the silky smooth skin over his impressive erection.

Now it was his turn to groan. "Stop." He put his hand

over hers and the sight of their fingers twined together caused something to break open in her heart.

He tugged her toward the bedroom. "I want room to explore."

Explore? That didn't sound like it was going to be fast or anytime soon.

She was dying. "I need you inside me."

"Let's see what we can do about that."

MARSH TUGGED her toward the bedroom. If he were honest, he had been wanting to do this since he had looked at the painting.

He was still stunned that she had managed to capture such beauty in their sexual interaction. He thought of sex as raw and earthy, but the lines and the colors of their painting also conveyed fluidity and grace.

Ayesha was impatient and within seconds *she* was leading *him* to the bedroom. He was harder than his Glock and loaded with an extra magazine. His cocked throbbed, bursting from his unzipped jeans like a divining rod. His own personal Ayesha pussy finder.

She let go of his hand and shimmied out of her leggings. He glanced down at the floor. "What is it with you and underwear?"

She giggled and crawled onto the bed, her sweater still hanging from her arms but her gorgeous ass presented for him.

Jesus. She was going to kill him. He wanted to take this slow.

He stepped toward the bed and caressed her ass with both palms. She moaned and pushed back into his touch.

Marsh watched with lazy appreciation, skimming his thumbs over the curve of her ass, moving ever so slowly toward the plump glistening lips of her sex. Dark curls framed her engorged maroon flesh.

Ayesha arched her back, pushing herself into his touch, and his thumb skimmed inside her.

Now it was his turn to moan. Her lips were slick with desire.

Shit. He had to do something or he was going to ram home without any finesse.

Marsh dropped to his knees and leaned close to her. "Spread your legs wider." His breath puffed against her quivering flesh.

"Praise Jesus." But she did as he requested.

Marsh ran his tongue along her inner thigh, inhaling her sweet musk. He licked up into the crease between her butt and her sex. His nose brushed her clit and she inhaled a quick breath.

"Please," she begged. And goddamn if that didn't turn him on even more. His cock leaked with pre-come.

He wanted to make this last for her. And for him. Because he knew without a doubt that it could be a while before this happened again. He never knew what she was going to do next.

Using his hands, he spread her wide and pressed the tip of his tongue against her clit and trilled. Then he lapped up her juices. He puckered his mouth and French kissed her sex, moving his tongue in and out. Her hips jerked in time to his kisses and she panted a litany of "Oh God, oh God."

Marsh closed his lips around her and sucked. He slid his palms beneath her sweater and pinched her nipples hard while he sucked on her clit.

Ayesha came with a keening wail. Her channel gripping

his tongue, trying desperately to suck him inside. He continued to tug on her nipples while he ate at her, trying to draw out her orgasm for as long as he could.

She collapsed on the bed, panting furiously. A rosy flush covered her ass and thighs. Marsh sat back on his heels, satisfied with the sounds of her orgasm.

She lay there for only about fifteen seconds, then she pushed up on her elbows and turned her head so he could see her face. Her pupils were blown and her hair curled around her face. "Get inside me. Now."

He could get on board with that. He shoved off his jeans, pulled a condom from his wallet, and rolled it over his painful erection. "Hold on."

She gripped the comforter in her fists as he clasped his hands around her hips and slammed home. Sensation overwhelmed him. His head literally went weak as he banged against her sex. Her vagina swallowed him whole and sucked him in. She pushed back as he thrust into her, his balls banging against her sex until they were both grunting. He had wanted to make this last but that wasn't going to happen.

His cock got even harder and his vision grayed as he pumped into her. He came in a blast, pumping his come into the condom. She slammed back against him, and even though he was coming, he forced himself to focus and slipped one hand around to her front and squeezed her clit.

Ayesha came again, her body pulsing around his cock as they flew off the edge together. His orgasm was like an explosion of colors bursting in his brain, filling his vision, and rendering him spent.

Marsh leaned over her body and gripped her fists with his palms, twining their fingers together. He pressed a line of kisses down her neck. He eased out of her and rolled to the side, pulling her with him so they could spoon on the bed. He figured he didn't have long, but he was going to give her the tenderness he'd been trying for earlier.

He would take whatever time she was willing to give him. What they shared transcended anything he'd ever experienced. And he never wanted to let her go.

Chapter 13

Tonight was the night.

In more ways than one.

Ayesha was nervous. She had been working toward this
moment for six months. But now, her focus was entirely on
the job happening hundreds of miles away. She had planned
everything as well as she could, and tonight was the first
step. If anything went wrong, she was screwed.

She rubbed damp palms over her knees as she sat in
Marsh's back seat. They had picked up her grandfather on
the way to her show opening. She had ended up with that
bodyguard anyway.

She should probably feel awkward because they had
slept together again after the interview. But she wasn't sorry.
Truth: the emotion that dominated her when she was with
Marsh was shame. She hated that she was lying to him. He
would hate that. Of course, because she was using him, they
had no hope of a future. But he didn't know that. Because
even though her heart wanted a chance with him, how
could she enter a relationship built on lies? And she could
never tell him the truth.

If Marsh ever found out what she'd done, he would hate her. Her Gramps had to come first. He was the most important person in her life.

Her Gramps was worth more to her than some fleeting sexual relationship.

Even if it didn't feel like it was only sexual. Even if it felt like it could be more than just fleeting. Perhaps if they'd met under different circumstances… If they'd met in some alternate universe where he wasn't former law enforcement and she wasn't about to become a criminal.

It was bitter cold tonight. The snap had come on suddenly and her light wool wrap was no barrier against the frigid temperatures. As if Marsh were attuned to her, he turned up the heat.

She shivered in the back seat. "Thank you."

"I'm proud of you, girl." Gramps piped up from the front seat.

"Thanks, Gramps."

"She's been a prodigy since she was ten."

"Marsh doesn't want to hear about my paint by numbers when I was a kid." She'd prefer he didn't hear about her painting evolution at all.

"Pure genius." Gramps's voice was thin and wavery.

"I'm looking forward to seeing all of your work," Marsh said from the driver's seat.

Ayesha squirmed. "This is my least favorite part. I don't know why I need to be there."

"People want to meet the artist. But you'll be protected."

There hadn't been any more attempts to hurt or scare her. Thank goodness. She was pretty sure that Marsh had someone watching her. She'd finally given up worrying about it and focused on painting.

"I've got myself and Viktor." His gaze flashed to hers in the rearview mirror. "You remember him."

The guy she had ditched. She nodded.

"We'll keep an eye on the patrons. And I have one other person who will be disguised in the crowd."

Ayesha snorted. "Crowd?"

Whatever you want to call it. She's undercover."

"Are we expecting trouble?" Gramps asked. The concern in his voice was evident.

She placed her hand on her grandfather's shoulder. "Purely precautionary."

"How are you feeling?" Marsh asked her grandfather.

"I wouldn't miss this for the world."

Not an answer. Which Marsh also seemed to pick up on.

"Well, if at any time you feel like you need to go home, I will arrange it."

Over her dead body. Of course she couldn't tell Marsh that. She needed her grandfather to have a solid alibi for when the fakes were being removed from the dead Harrington's Cape Cod home.

She would cross that bridge if needed.

"I did a security check earlier. And everything seems in-line and good to go," Marsh said. "Gallery owner hasn't noticed any irregularities."

He was in his protection mode. His whole body on high alert. Even the way he drove the car was more intense, more aware. He changed lanes smoothly and drove past the gallery.

Promise Lewis had gone all out. The interior was lit up like a beacon glowing and standing out among all the other shops on the street. Urns with small twinkle lights flanked the double glass doors. Her art sat on giant easels in the windows, displayed alone with a single light shining down on her work. Groups of people mingled inside.

He drove past the entrance. "I'm taking you around to the back."

Ayesha craned her head to stare at the turnout. "Okay."

In a few minutes, they were parked at the rear entrance to the gallery. Ayesha went to open her car door and a face appeared, startling her. She yelped. Then realized it was Marsh's guy, Viktor. He opened the back door and held out his hand slowly. She placed her hand in his and let him ease her out of the sedan.

"Sorry I startled you."

"Not your fault. I'm a little on edge." Everyone would assume it was because of the show, only she knew the truth.

He nodded once and slammed the door shut. Then he proceeded to help Gramps out of the car.

"You're on point until I can park," Marsh said.

Viktor nodded once and held out his arm for her Gramps. The proud old man hesitated a second before he grasped Viktor's elbow. They headed into the gallery and Ayesha took a moment to let it sink in. This was her largest gallery showing yet. And the first where she was the headliner.

She had the most pieces at ten and the other four artists each had five.

Partitioned white walls separated the large room into smaller, more intimate spaces. The lacquered wood floor gleamed under the flattering lights, and guests mingled throughout the room, clustered around each featured painting with champagne flutes clutched in their hands.

Promise had moved things around. Somehow she had included Ayesha's line drawing of Marsh in the show. No one but her would know it was Marsh, but still a flush swelled through her.

The atmosphere reminded her of the lavish parties her parents used to throw and her hatred of being paraded around for viewing until she'd acted out so much that her mother let her skip the functions. But if she wanted to be a success, then she had to get over the stage fright roiling her stomach.

Viktor turned to her and crooked his elbow. "You ready?"

Ayesha took a deep breath. As she'd ever be.

"You've got this. Anybody who can ditch me will be fine."

And again, she thought, *not a PR firm.*

MARSH PARKED the car and headed for the gallery, feeling an unexpected sense of optimism.

He studied the exterior of the building, looking for any threats. Adams-Larsen had done a security sweep earlier in the day. Viktor and Jake had done a thorough assessment of the property, checking out all the exits and entrances, windows, doors and the fire escape. It was as safe as it could be without completely vetting the guest list—which was impossible.

Marsh had begun to let down his guard since nothing had happened lately. There'd been no other attempts to hurt or scare Ayesha. However, that could be to the due to the fact that either he or Jake or Viktor had been watching her condo.

He walked into the art gallery. Their large canvas was the main focal point of the exhibit. Once again, he was mesmerized by the passionate couple on the canvas. He smoothed his hand over his tuxedo front and hoped no one caught his flash of embarrassment. He wasn't a prude. The nakedness didn't bother him. It was the raw emotion conveyed in the painting that caused his throat to tighten.

He had feelings for this woman, and he was going to have to resolve them. But that could wait until tonight was over.

He touched the earpiece and murmured, "Exterior looks good. Check-in."

"Back door, fine," Viktor said.

"I'm going to need the recipe for these cheese puffs," said Maria.

Marsh snorted. "I'll see what I can do."

He was still getting to know Maria. She'd come to ALIAS as a client when he'd been out of touch. She was amazingly resilient. She'd survived being a prisoner for over eight years. One of the things she had discovered in the past few months—besides the love of their own version of the Rock, operative Dwayne Lameko—was a love of cooking. She'd been experimenting regularly and bringing all sorts of goodies into the office.

She'd proven herself on an op a few months ago, but she was still learning the business. She was an amazingly quick study and tonight was the perfect learning opportunity.

He and Maria moved through the crowd easily, keeping on opposite sides of the room. He continued to monitor the door and the patrons, making sure no one was getting out of hand. He had settled into protection mode with a simplistic ease. The routines and motions came back easily. The entire time he watched the crowd, he kept one eye on Ayesha. Her smile was as fake as the leather dress she wore. It warmed something inside to realize that she reserved a special smile just for him.

Marsh also kept Lincoln Brown in his sights. The older man seemed fragile, as if a strong wind would blow him over. "Keep an eye on Lincoln Brown." They might need to remove him early.

In his other ear, he was listening to the comms for ALIAS team two. They had managed to obtain a charter flight to Cape Cod earlier than expected and were in the process of removing the two paintings from the Harrington estate now.

"How's it going, Jillian?"

"Not a problem in sight." He could hear the rustling of their clothing. "We've got the paintings secured in their crates. Confirmed that the RFID beacons are working. We are tuned into their frequency, as is the insurance company. Everyone is monitoring their progress so that the chain of custody is never broken."

Excellent.

"Headed to the airport now. Should be back in DC within a couple of hours. I'll let you know when the paintings are secured in the vault."

One problem down. Maybe tonight was going to go off without a hitch.

It was as if he'd tempted fate. "Shit."

"What's wrong?" Jill asked.

"Harrington's son just walked into this show."

"And that's a problem because…?"

"There's something between Lincoln Brown and the Harrington son." And Marsh didn't like it. Harrington moved around the crowd as if he were the host. Shaking hands, clapping people on the back, acting jovially.

Something about the guy's demeanor set off Marsh's radar.

"Kita didn't find much of anything beyond some business dealings."

"It's there. It must be hidden." When Harrington made his way to Lincoln Brown, Marsh moved to the outside of the room and edged around until he was near enough to overhear part of their conversation.

"Quite the turnout," Harrington said.

"I'm very proud of my girl." Lincoln Brown didn't look at Harrington but kept his eyes on Ayesha.

"I know that you are."

Harrington leaned closer and whispered something to Lincoln Brown, but Marsh couldn't hear him. His attention had been fractured by the newest arrivals to the show.

"What the hell are they doing here together?"

"Problem?" Jill echoed in one ear and Viktor in the other.

"It's my parents." Marsh knew he should be paying attention to Lincoln Brown, but he was stuck on the entrance, where his mother and father had come in. *Together.*

"They are adults," Jill said with a laugh in her voice. She was getting back at him.

"I am aware. I just would prefer that they weren't adults in front of me." Marsh stalked to his parents, doing a quick check on Ayesha, who had another fake smile plastered on her face as she spoke with an older white couple in front of what he'd come to think of as *their* painting.

Marsh was losing his mind, feeling possessive of a canvas and paint. "Viktor, you keep eyes on the crowd. I'll only be a minute."

"Marsh, darling. How are you?" His mother gave him a

giant hug. He held on for second, feeling guilty because she had called several times and he hadn't called her back.

He disengaged from his mother. "I'm fine."

His father eyed him warily.

"What are you doing here?"

"We came to support Ayesha." His mother smiled brightly. "I do love her work."

His father just nodded at him. "Thank you."

He wanted to grump at his father but that would be real mature. Marsh just nodded as well.

"Where is the woman of the hour?"

Marsh dragged his gaze away from his parents and looked around the gallery again. He didn't see Ayesha.

And Harrington was also in the wind.

"Viktor. Eyes on our protectee?"

"She didn't go out the back door."

"She went to the restroom." Maria piped up.

"Maria, follow her." He didn't like that he couldn't see Harrington.

"Got her," Maria said in his ear. "Everything's fine."

Marsh relaxed.

"Listen, sweetie." Uh oh, something bad was coming. His mother only called him sweetie when she had a request that he wasn't going to like.

Ayesha had exited the tiny bathroom in the back corner and Maria followed behind her. While he trusted Maria, he still didn't see Harrington. He was only half paying attention when she said, "I'd like to do a family brunch tomorrow for Christmas Eve."

"Sure," he said absently. And then her words registered. "What family?"

"You, me, and your father. Kita if she isn't spending the

time with Alex's family, and Jillian as well. I know it's last minute…."

He was stuck on the fact that for the first time in twenty years, his father and mother were planning on being in the same room for part of the holiday celebration.

"He's going to be there?" Marsh couldn't look at his father.

"Yes." His father finally spoke up. "Your mother and I are trying to—"

Please God, do not say reconcile.

"Mend our relationship."

"Mend, how?"

"For God's sake, she's forgiven me. We're just trying to be a family. To spend some time with our son together."

"So you aren't getting back together?"

His mother flushed. "Ah, no."

But something was up. "Then what?"

"I…ah, have a new friend."

Marsh watched Ayesha work the room, but her heart wasn't in it. Something had happened between the beginning of the night and now. He needed to know what. "That's nice," he said absently.

"Got to admit, I thought that would be a bit more of an issue," his dad said heartily.

Wait, what did his mom just say? "A friend." He blinked.

"Ah, yes. And I'd like you to meet him."

Blindsided. That's how Marsh felt right this moment. It was as if he'd disappeared for a few months and everyone had moved on without him.

"Ah, okay." *I guess.*

It would have to be okay. But Jesus, that was something he didn't really want to think about.

"And are you planning on spending tomorrow night at my house or your condo?" She flushed again.

Dear God in heaven, she didn't want him spending the night at her house. He'd rather be with Ayesha anyway. Assuming she'd have him.

"I won't be at home." Marsh glanced over at Lincoln Brown. "Good chat. I'll see you tomorrow."

His mother rattled off a time and he left them to it.

Marsh moved over to Lincoln Brown. The older man looked more frail than he had a few minutes ago. "You doing okay, Linc?"

"Don't worry about me." Lincoln Brown waved a shaky hand toward where Ayesha had been standing. "You promise me you'll look out for her."

"Absolutely. I won't let anything happen to her," Marsh said fiercely.

"I'm glad she's got you as a protector."

"Maybe it's time we got you home."

As if his words had conjured her, Ayesha was right next to them. "He's fine," she insisted.

"My girl's right. I'll just hang out here on this lovely sofa and people watch."

"It's no problem. We can have Viktor take you home."

"No, I want him to stay until the end."

And right there, Marsh's satisfaction with the night crumbled. She could see that her grandfather was visibly tiring. The man she claimed to love needed rest. So why didn't she want him to leave this gallery? She wanted them both covered would be his guess. He leaned closer and narrowed his gaze at her. Then he murmured in her ear, "Alibis?"

Her flinch was barely there. If he hadn't been expressly looking for it, he would have missed her reaction. He knew he hit the nail on the head. But why would she need an alibi for a sanctioned removal of the estate's paintings?

He'd forgotten that Jill could hear him as well.

"What are you talking about?" Jill said sharply. Just as Ayesha said, "Not at all. My Gramps deserves the recognition for tonight just as much as I do. He's the one I owe everything to."

There was a message in that statement. But something else was going on and he was going to figure out what she was hiding.

"Nothing important," he replied to Jill. Then he covered the small microphone and said to Ayesha, "We're going to talk about this later."

"Sure." She smiled vacantly, the fake smile and he hated it.

"I'll text you when the paintings are secured in the vault. Then I'm headed to Scotland." Jillian's voice was calm, at ease.

"That's awfully fast." She had just met Hamish a few weeks ago. Marsh's protective instincts fired to life.

"When you know, you know."

That's what he was afraid of.

Chapter 14

A light dusting of snow had fallen overnight, along with the temperature. Marsh strode up the walkway to his family home, dreading the next few hours.

He was here to meet his mother's…boyfriend? And so weird, his father was going to be here too.

The Christmas tree lights were on, blinking merrily in the gray morning. He'd get through this Christmas Eve brunch and then maybe he could track down Ayesha. She'd managed to avoid a discussion last night by staying with her grandfather. He'd dropped them at the elder Brown's house and she'd shooed him on his way.

He trudged up the wide welcoming steps. Everything looked the same as the last time he had been here just a few days ago, but everything was different.

His personal life was in such a mess. Maybe the fact his mother had a boyfriend wouldn't be so disconcerting, but Marsh felt like his entire life was shifting on its axis.

He knocked and then used his key.

His father sat in a wing chair by the fire, sipping a cup of coffee.

"Marsh!" His mother rushed in from the kitchen and patted him on the arm. "Come in and take off your coat."

He looked around curiously, wondering if the boyfriend was here yet.

"Do you want something to drink?"

"I'm good." Marsh shrugged out of his coat and hung it on a peg in the mudroom off the kitchen. He glanced at his watch and wondered how long he needed to stay. But mixed with that impatience was a certain nostalgia. The kitchen was scented with their traditional Christmas Eve brunch. An egg casserole with sausage and cheese, sweet cinnamon rolls that his mother made from scratch, and a bowl of fresh berries were set out on the antique maple sideboard. Coffee laced with peppermint schnapps steamed in a silver carafe, and a can of whipped cream sat on the kitchen counter.

"Harold should be here soon."

Harold. Okay this was getting more real. He grabbed the can of whipped cream tilted his head back and gave himself a shot.

"Marshall Winston Adams."

"Sorry, Mom," he said through a mouthful of whip cream.

"Hand it over." His mom held out her hand and he slapped the can in it. But instead of putting it back on the counter, she took her own shot.

Marsh swallowed a laugh. "Mom."

"I'm trying new things on for size."

Back in the living room, his father laughed. "I'll say you are."

His mother flushed.

This easy camaraderie between them was odd.

"That's great, Mom," he said. "But what is he doing here?"

"Your father is the one who introduced me to Harold."

"We met in our weekly hiking group."

His father had a weekly hiking group? As if he'd heard Marsh, his father said, "We take hikes in the parks around the DC area, looking at birds and exploring the parks. Like you and I used to do."

That brought back memories Marsh had shoved into the recesses of his brain. On Saturday mornings, they would give his mom a break and head out to the park. He and his father would walk along the paths, stopping to peer into the creek and watch for fish and ducks. In the spring, they'd spend extra time watching the fuzzy little ducklings follow their mother around. He'd bring home leaves and twigs, little treasures for his mother, and his father would gather up his mother in a big hug when they returned.

Moisture pricked his eyes as those memories flooded back in.

But that didn't negate what his father had done. He ignored his father and focused on his mother. A boyfriend. Having a name made the guy seem more real. Harold. "They're friends?"

"Old friends."

He couldn't wrap his head around that. "Maybe you two can double date."

He meant for the words to be snarky, but his mother never did what he expected these days. "Maybe we will. Of course your father would have to decide which floozy to bring."

Floozy?

"But that's old business." His mother squeezed his biceps. "It's time you and your father forgave each other."

"Forgave each other?" That pissed him off. "I'm the one who needs to forgive."

But in his head, he knew that he had made mistakes as well. The melancholy that filled him with all three of them back in his childhood home was a bitter pill.

His phone buzzed. Saved.

He pulled it out and looked at the display. "I have to take this."

She sighed heavily. His mother wasn't happy with him. And he knew he was spoiling her moment, but Jake wouldn't call unless it was an emergency.

"What's up?"

Jake was in the booth today. He'd offered to take both Christmas Eve and Christmas since he didn't have any family in town. "You wanted me to call you if she was on the move."

She. Maybe she was doing some shopping.

"It looks like she's heading toward Virginia."

Virginia? Marsh thought back to the research she'd done at the library and he wondered if that was where she was going. "Can you hook my phone up to her GPS readings so I can follow her?"

"Absolutely."

"Thanks." Marsh pushed the off button on his phone.

His mother stood in the middle of her kitchen, a frown on her face and frustration coating her features.

"I have to go."

His mother hugged him tight and whispered, "You have to fix this."

"I can't right now." Marsh shoved his phone in his pocket and headed for the front door. But the look on her face stopped him. "I'm sorry. This is important."

"So is your relationship with your father."

Even though it curdled his stomach, he promised her. "Later."

"Will you come back?"

"If I can." But his mind was already on whatever Ayesha was doing.

He stopped by the **ALIAS** garage and picked up one of their decoy cars. They used these nondescript Honda Accords for client transportation when they were trying to hide their movements.

This way she wouldn't recognize his car tailing her.

Forty minutes later, he had almost caught up to her. Luckily she'd been doing the posted speed limit and he had been hauling ass.

"We have any idea if she's driving or taking a ride share service?"

"Nothing showed up on her credit cards. And she hasn't activated her app. I'm not really sure."

He had felt a little guilty tracking her. But now he was really glad that he had gone ahead and done it anyway. They were headed into a residential area of old stately homes with carriage houses and large lawns. One or two houses were straight-up castles. The neighborhood was decked out for the holidays with garland and lights and cutesy decorations on top of their mailboxes. Marsh studied the path she was taking. He was pretty sure she was headed to the coordinates of the house she'd researched at the library. What the hell was she up to?

He had marked the spot on his phone, but he hadn't followed through to find out whose house it was. Now he was kicking himself. But there'd been a million things going on and this had slipped through the cracks.

The streets were mostly deserted. Luxury cars lined the driveways of the houses with guests. Other houses were lit up with lights, fake candles in every window, and large

Christmas trees in giant picture windows, but little evidence anyone was home.

He finally caught up to her. She was driving a late model minivan. Not the standard car of most of these residents, who leaned more toward Range Rovers and Mercedes M-class SUVs. But it also didn't stand out. He'd bet most of the staff in these parts drove cars like the one she was driving.

He could see her hair in the rearview. He wondered if this was like before and she wouldn't notice that she was being followed.

She drove past the house in question and turned left at the next street. Marsh followed behind her. Snow was beginning to fall in big fat flakes, giving the entire area a very Norman Rockwell vibe. He dropped back so that she wouldn't catch on to him. At the next road, she turned left again. And he was pretty sure that this was the back of the house that she'd researched. He'd had Viktor give him the schematics and there was a garage on the back of the property. She drove straight up to the garage, and within moments the garage door began to rise.

Since he was damn sure she wasn't the owner and neither was her family, she must have obtained a cloned door opener.

Marsh parked his car along the back hedgerow and followed her stealthily. She moved confidently as if she knew exactly what she was doing and where she was going. She slung a large leather bag over her shoulder. She was just about to close the garage door when he spoke.

"What the hell are you doing?"

AYESHA WHIRLED AROUND, her eyes wide and her pulse pounding in her throat as Marsh Adams stepped into Harrington's garage.

"You scared me half to death." But then she stopped. "What are you doing here? And how did you find me?"

"The better question would be what are you doing here?"

At that she paused. Shit. She just looked at him and wondered…could she trust him? And did she have a choice? He was going to hate her. Which she'd have to live with, as long as he didn't try and stop her.

She needed to close the garage door before some well-meaning neighbor spotted the van that didn't belong. She pressed the remote and the door rumbled, closing slowly in the tense silence.

"Whose house is this?"

"Harrington the Fourth's." Her heart beat so hard it threatened to pound out of her chest. He could turn her in. But the reality was she had to get the original paintings out of Harrington's house or her Gramps would be in trouble.

"Explain to me why you're here," he said again.

She took a deep breath. She knew that as soon as she explained, any hope of a future was gone. Realistically she'd known that before but she never thought she would actually have to tell him what she had done. "I'm here to steal the original paintings."

Marsh blinked. Opened his mouth. Closed his mouth. "The *original* paintings?"

"We don't have time to talk about it here." She rubbed a shaky hand over hair. She'd been mentally counting down the seconds. She had limited time to get this done. "I've got to get moving."

He studied her, a look of pure betrayal on his face. He finally opened his mouth and she braced for the censure she knew was coming. But all he asked was, "Are you sure he isn't home?"

"Yes. He's at a family brunch. They have it every year at his sister's house in DC." Her stomach revolted. She couldn't afford to get sick. Later she could puke to her heart's desire.

"If he has the originals, what did we remove from Cape Cod yesterday?"

"Forgeries."

"You have a lot of explaining to do."

"Later," she implored him.

"How are you planning to get in?"

The dim lighting in the garage made it hard for her to see his face but his anger throbbed in the space between them.

"There's a tunnel between the garage and the house. "

"Security?"

"There's no alarm system for the garage or the entrance to the house from the tunnel, because no one is supposed to know it's there."

"Then how do you know?"

"I can't tell you." She couldn't give up her grandfather. "You need to go."

She was desperate for him to leave. Typically Harrington spent a good portion of the day at his sister's home. But she needed to get in and out, just in case his schedule changed.

"I'm coming with you."

"You should just go." She didn't want him to do anything that jeopardized his conscience.

"You want me to leave?"

"Yes. I've got this."

"You have a lot of experience breaking into houses?"

"Of course not!" she cried. "But you don't want to be a part of this."

"You need my help."

"I don't need it." But she sure wouldn't mind the assist.

"So fucking stubborn." He shook his head. "Let's go."

AYESHA FUMBLED WITH LOCK PICKS, her hands shaking. Marsh silently watched, wondering how she knew what to do. Finally the lock clicked and she opened the door to the underground tunnel. They descended the stairs in silence, and motion sensor lights blinked on as they made their way to the house. The distance between the house and the garage was about a quarter of a mile. They paused at intervals to listen for any indication that they had been discovered. The air was stuffy and tense.

"What about guards?" Marsh snapped out.

"Too much of a cheapskate."

"Dogs?"

"I have some laced dog treats in case we need them. But typically the dogs are kenneled when no one is home. They're strictly for patrolling the grounds when the family is in residence."

"And where are the paintings?"

"If my information is correct, he keeps them in a hidden room under the main staircase. It may be disguised as a bookshelf."

"It looks like you thought of everything." But his words weren't a compliment.

Marsh stalked beside Ayesha. The sense of betrayal

caught him off guard. What was he even doing here? Except he knew the answer.

Now all those furtive discussions made sense. Harrington the Fourth had been threatening Ayesha's grandfather. "What happens if we turn around and go back?"

"Jonathon Harrington will accuse my grandfather of stealing his father's paintings. And the paintings that were taken from the estate will be exposed as forgeries. Forgeries that my grandfather authenticated fifteen years ago."

Fifteen years ago. "When you were thirteen?"

She stopped in her tracks. Then she shook her head and started again. They didn't have time to waste.

Everything came back to when Ayesha was thirteen. He still hadn't put it all together but if Jonathon Harrington the Fourth had the original paintings in his house then he knew he was in possession of stolen merchandise.

"Why not just let the authorities know that Harrington has the originals and he stole them from his father?"

"That would implicate other people."

Other people being her grandfather. Shit.

Betrayal burned beneath his breastbone. She had used him. Used ALIAS to do her dirty work. But even if he left her to this, ALIAS would once again be in the news. He had no choice but to help her pull this off.

Otherwise his friends and his company would pay the price. He would let down Jillian and Kita and everyone else at ALIAS. They were more than just his coworkers, more like his family than friends. He couldn't let them down again.

But he was sick that his choices had once again led to the company being compromised. Even more so when he considered that he woman he'd been falling for was a liar and a thief.

They came to the entrance to the house. This would be the crucial moment. "You're sure there's no alarm on this door?"

"As sure as I can be." Her hands were shaking so badly she couldn't insert the picks into the doorknob. The security was laughable. It was a simple lock that could be purchased at the local hardware store. Harrington was one arrogant bastard.

Marsh opened his hand. "Give them to me."

She tentatively dropped the tools into his hand. "You could just go."

"Not a chance. If you get caught, ALIAS goes down with you."

If anything, she looked more miserable. But Marsh hardened his heart. She didn't deserve his sympathy.

He finessed the simple lock and the tumblers opened with a click. Ayesha inhaled slowly and then let it out.

"Let's do this." Marsh turned the knob and hoped for the best.

The door swung open and…nothing. Nothing happened. No dogs came running. No alarm started blaring. There wasn't even a keypad next to the door, which meant that her intel had been correct.

"Let's go." They needed to get in, get out, and get gone. He noticed that she was wearing gloves. Smart move. She flipped on the light switch and they headed up the stairs. Marsh realized he needed to wipe the doorknob down on his way out. Just in case Harrington was ballsy enough to report the theft.

At the top of the stairs, he looked for any kind of security keypad. But there was nothing.

He nodded to her. "You open the door."

She turned the doorknob cautiously and they peered

into what appeared to be a mudroom. A long bench with hooks on the wall above it and baskets below it graced one wall, and at the other end of the small room was a French door that led into the kitchen.

"From now on, proceed cautiously."

They got into the kitchen and headed for the entryway. The two-story entry was a statement in grandiosity. The middle of the room was open with a round table on a round rug and a giant centerpiece of poinsettias and birch sticks. Staircases on either side of the round room ascended to the second floor.

"You take that side, I'll take this one." Marsh started at the base of the stairs and looked for any kind of lever or seam that would indicate there was a hidden doorway or a secret room. He worked quickly but carefully, moving from the base of the stairs all the way to the entrance to the kitchen. But there was nothing. When he got to the end of his side, he looked at Ayesha. She shook her head slowly.

"Shit."

"Where did you get your information?"

"From my grandfather's notes," she said miserably.

"Maybe it's not this staircase. Maybe it's on the second floor. Let's check the next level." They quickly ascended the stairs and looked around. The house was separated into two wings.

"From now on we stick together." Marsh started the timer on his watch. "If we hit twenty minutes, we've got to get out of here."

It was still way too much time inside.

"Okay." Her answer was the most subdued he'd ever seen her. "Where do you think he'd keep them?"

"Near him." She headed down the hallway. "Let's check out the master bedroom." In the master bedroom they found a giant king-size four-poster bed, antique furnishings, and a wall of bookcases. There was also a circular stair up to a balcony that held a small sitting area full of bookshelves. They searched the bedroom but couldn't find any secret room.

When they got up to the sitting area, they started on opposite sides and again looked for any kind of seam or lever that might indicate a secret room. But there was nothing, and as he looked out the window, he realized there was no extra space, at least on this wall.

And when he looked out the window, he knew they had more problems.

"What's wrong?"

"It's snowing. Hard."

If Harrington decided to come back soon, they were in trouble. And if they didn't leave quickly, their cars would leave a trail a blind man could follow.

Marsh turned around and stared out at the two-story master bedroom from the balcony. He studied the lines of the room and realized that there might just be space behind the metal spiral staircase that led up to the balcony. "Hold on."

He hustled down the stairs and started looking at the wall behind the staircase. But as he searched for seam, he wondered how they would get into the secret room even if they found a seam.

"Wait." Ayesha closed her eyes and held up her hand as if mentally reviewing the blueprints. "I have an idea."

She started at one end of the curved wall behind the staircase and within minutes, she'd found it. "Here."

Marsh glanced at his watch. They had three minutes left. "Hurry."

She shifted the painting on the wall and it swung open,

revealing a small room. Lights went on as the motion was detected, and there along the wall were apparently two original Rembrandts and several other paintings, a modern one with lots of gold and another small landscape in an ornate frame.

"Let's get the paintings and go."

"We've got to see if he's got RFID tags on them."

"The guy who has no security anywhere?"

"He put the tags on his father's paintings."

"Fine. But make it quick."

Ayesha ran her fingers over the frame of the first picture, a landscape in muted colors. It wasn't even that large. "Got it."

She lifted the picture off the wall and carefully removed the painting from its frame. She handed it to him. "There's a soft museum-grade fabric to wrap it in, inside the bag."

While Marsh wrapped the first painting, she removed the second one, a portrait, from its frame. He wrapped it carefully and then they slid the paintings in the large bag she'd brought to carry them. She hefted the bag over her shoulder.

Marsh studied the carrying bag. "It's not optimal."

"I don't care. Let's get out of here." Ayesha nodded and they exited the room and quickly closed the secret door.

"Give it to me," he demanded.

"I've got it."

"It's heavy and I can move faster. We need to get out of here," Marsh said. He was pissed and they still weren't out of danger yet.

She grudgingly handed him the bag. That meant he was in possession of stolen merchandise which pissed him off all over again.

He glanced out the window and swore. The weather had dumped a ton of snow in the past thirty minutes.

They hustled out of the master and down the stairs, not running but walking at a fast pace. Every second they were inside this house was a second that they could be discovered.

When they got through the kitchen they must have made too much noise.

The rough bark of Dobermans hit his eardrums, scaring the shit out of him. "Go. Go."

"They can't get loose."

"For all you know he has some sort of noise alarm. Let's get the fuck out of here."

They ran down the tunnel, the strap of the bag digging into Marsh's shoulder. When they got to the garage, he demanded the keys. "I'm driving. Get in the van."

She started to argue.

Marsh ignored her and held out his hand.

She slapped the keys into his palm and headed to the passenger seat.

He started the engine while the garage door was rolling up and then slowly backed out of the garage as if he had all the time in the world.

When he got to the end of the street, he turned and drove past the Honda. He pulled out his cell and speed dialed Jake.

"Everything okay?"

"I need you to double check that the Honda can't be traced back to ALIAS."

"We're good," Jake replied slowly.

"Okay, thanks. Can you put Viktor on call?" Marsh accelerated slowly, keeping within in the speed limit, and headed toward the highway. "We may have a situation."

"Done."

"Thanks." Marsh jabbed the off button and finally shot a glance at the silent Ayesha. "Where to?"

Chapter 15

Ayesha sat in the passenger seat trying to feel victorious. She had pulled it off! But it was difficult with Marsh's animosity directed at her.

She didn't blame him. At all.

The silent ride was filled with acrimony. The trip to her grandfather's studio and vault felt like it took forever.

They pulled up to the back of the nondescript warehouse in an industrial area of town. On Christmas Eve, the block was deserted. Perfect time to move the paintings.

Marsh put the van in park next to the rear entrance to the warehouse. "How are we getting into the building?"

"The back door."

"We don't want a record of our entry and exit."

"Oh." Shit. She hadn't even thought about that.

"Hold on." Marsh punched a number in his cell phone.

"What are you doing?"

"Getting help from my team."

"But no one is supposed to know we've done this."

"Sorry but that's not how this is going to work."

"This?" Ayesha stuttered, her heart thundering.

"ALIAS's involvement."

"I told you to walk away." Yes, she felt guilty right now. But what the hell? "You have no right."

"You made this my business when you used ALIAS to carry out your plan." Marsh's hand was tight on his phone, his knuckles white. "I am not about to betray my partner and my friends by keeping this a secret."

He said into his phone, "Hey Kita. I need a quick favor. Can you hack into Lincoln Brown's office security system and disable it without setting it off?"

Ayesha's stomach turned. Sweat gathered under her armpits and along her hairline.

Marsh hesitated. "I'll explain later."

He hung up the phone. "We're a go."

They left the van parked at the back of the alley in the industrial area. The entire neighborhood was deserted in the early afternoon on Christmas Eve.

Marsh bypassed the security system and they hustled into the back door of her grandfather's studio and storage facility.

"What's the plan?"

"Follow me." She headed for the vault in the back of the room. She hadn't been here in years and a sense of nostalgia hit her out of the blue.

She opened the vault quickly after entering the alphanumeric password.

Motion sensitive lights blinked on illuminating the small room with a bright ambient light.

The room was six feet deep and about ten feet wide. A low cabinet of shallow drawers was set up like a morgue along the long wall. There were enough drawers to hold approximately twenty small or ten large paintings. Although not everyone had Gramps appraise their work in his studio and the case was rarely full anymore.

A long table in front of the storage drawers was wide enough to accommodate even the larger paintings. Fortunately, both the Rembrandts were relatively small.

"All those drawers hold priceless paintings?"

"Sometimes. But Gramps does restoration work as well as appraisals and they are rarely as expensive as these. If fine motor skills are needed he has colleagues who will come in for that skill. His hands shake too much nowadays."

Ayesha opened the drawer with the portrait and slowly, carefully removed the fake painting from the ornate frame. Marsh stood silently by, a sentinel for this final act. She slipped the original painting back into the frame it had been housed in before her grandfather had facilitated its theft years ago.

Her heart beat a staccato rhythm as she studied the fake.

"I can't tell the difference." Marsh's voice from behind her startled her. She'd been lost in contemplation. Objectively, the paint had been layered on thick and dark, exactly like the originals. "There are subtle differences in the fakes, but it would take an expert to see them."

Or an expert to certify them. She shuddered.

"Everything okay?" Marsh asked.

"Rembrandt was known for his self-portraits." She trailed a finger over the gilt frame. "There are at least forty known paintings still in existence."

She discarded the fake on the long table and moved to replace the second painting, a pastoral landscape showing a woman kneeling in the garden with a basket of herbs at her feet.

She quickly and efficiently removed the landscape from its frame and replaced the second fake with the original.

After both drawers were shut, she stared at the fakes lying on the cold industrial table.

Marsh had been mostly quiet up until this point.

"Walk it through for me. What's going to happen when the paintings are appraised on the 26th?"

"My grandfather will verify that these were painted by Rembrandt, he'll test the paint and possibly the canvas, and the estate will get their tax write off."

"Everything above reproach." Marsh finished, "And the chain of custody will not have been broken because according to the RFID trackers, those paintings have been in the vault the entire time."

"Yes," she said miserably.

"It's smart."

"Thank you."

"What are you going to do with the fakes?"

She hesitated, her hands hovering over the two forgeries. "They need to be destroyed."

"How?"

Ayesha sighed. "The building has an incinerator." Resolutely she picked up the paintings. It was time. She closed and locked the vault.

She took one last glance around the restoration area. "This is where I started painting." Her gaze touched on the rows of paint tubes and brushes. Easels with paintings in various stages of restoration lined one wall. A metal architect's desk in the corner held official rubber stamps and ink pads. Gramps' ancient large desktop monitor was shoved into the corner. Authentication and provenance documents were still done with paper and pen.

So many memories. Some good. Some really, really bad.

WITH THE FAKE paintings concealed in the bag they'd used to transport the originals, Marsh followed Ayesha down the stairs and tried to get a bead on her mood.

He should be pissed. Okay, he was pissed. But something more was going on here and he couldn't figure it out.

The basement was dark with water-stained concrete and rusty support beams. A large incinerator in the corner belched heat. The fire was strong when Ayesha opened the hatch.

She stared into the hole, a weird look on her face. What was she waiting for?

Marsh glanced at his watch. They had already been here for over half an hour. Someone might notice the strange van in the alley. "We need to get going."

"You're right." She took a deep breath, closed her eyes, and tossed them in.

The paint and canvas reacted to the fire giving off a flare of bright colors. He pushed the door closed and grabbed her hand. It was the first time he'd touched her since he'd realized her betrayal. He should be disgusted, but when her hand trembled in his, concern was his overriding emotion.

Those tiny tremors were so unlike her normal bold personality. He guessed grand theft was reason enough for the strange vibes.

"What's going to happen when Harrington figures out that his originals have been stolen?"

"He's going to come after my grandfather."

"Then we need to be ready for him." Marsh hesitated another second.

"We?"

He was beyond pissed at her. But he still wouldn't leave her to deal with Harrington on her own. "Yeah."

Marsh made sure the building alarm was set. "This is secure?" About the only thing worse than the fact that they stole they originals was if someone else stole them from this building.

"Contrary to popular fiction, most art theft is a crime of opportunity. And once the paintings are stolen, if they are famous, they are really hard to unload."

Except…"Not always though." Since the paintings they'd just replaced had been stolen twice, technically.

She glanced at the smokestack on top of the building, puffing out a plume of black smoke. "Not always."

"What were you going to do if you got caught?"

"Wing it?" she said weakly.

"No plan in place?" Admonition grated his voice. "That was reckless and irresponsible."

"I'd always heard you were easygoing." Ayesha stomped toward the van. "Where is that guy?"

She really wanted to get into this right now? He wanted to shake her for being so flippant. The only other person who made him this angry was his father and his blatant disregard for other people's feelings, for his feelings. She'd gutted him with this betrayal. "Yeah, I am easygoing as long as I'm not breaking the law. That makes me pretty damn uptight."

"Yeah, well art theft is not in my regular repertoire either." Ayesha yanked open the door to the van. "I'm a little out of my element."

But she'd hesitated. What was that all about?

He'd have to figure it out later. He had one more call to make.

Marsh punched some numbers on his cell and waited for someone to answer.

"Kuznets."

"Viktor, I need you to set us up with some recording equipment, stat."

"Ten-four." He paused for a moment, then said, "Where do you need me?"

Marsh rattled off Lincoln Brown's address.

"Be there in twenty."

The shit was about to hit the fan.

"HOW LONG DO WE HAVE?" Marsh asked.

She knew exactly what he meant. "Typically, their Christmas Eve brunch lasts until three p.m. He comes home, presumably sloshed."

"And how long do you think it will take before he figures out the paintings are gone?"

"Half an hour, an hour, tops."

"Okay, so we have enough time to set up our comms and get ready."

"What are you going to do?"

"Harrington won't put himself in a position to be recorded so he will come in person."

"My thoughts as well." Her stomach tipped and rolled. What was done was done. And no matter what happened, Harrington the Fourth wouldn't get his hands on those paintings. Her Gramps was safe.

Until now, she hadn't realized how Marsh had looked at her before, with benevolence, with a sweetness and an acceptance that was now gone.

She had killed it. But the truth was she still wouldn't change what she'd done because she would do everything to protect her Gramps.

Chapter 16

They had dropped off the van and Viktor had picked them up in another nondescript Honda. The ride to Lincoln Brown's house was sullen and fraught with tension.

Marsh'd left Ayesha in the library while he and Viktor conferred in the kitchen. Her grandfather was taking a nap and hopefully wouldn't wake up until after it was all over. She'd confessed that she purposely kept him in the dark about her plans. But he would know something was up if he came downstairs and found Marsh and Viktor here.

"We'll be ready for him."

Marsh paced Lincoln's living room. The walls were lined with built-in bookshelves in some dark expensive wood. The chairs looked to be antiques. The liquor on the cart in the corner was top shelf.

"Why would your grandfather do something like that when he has all of this?" Marsh waved to the opulent room.

"This house is my mother's. Her family has a lot of money. My dad's not so much." A queasy look crossed her face. "And what happened was a long time ago. Harrington basically blackmailed him the last time."

They were waiting for Harrington to show up. Marsh refused to leave them alone. Even though he was angry with both of them.

"Don't take it out on my grandfather, he didn't know what I was going to do."

"He had to know you'd do something. He raised you."

Viktor had set them up. They were all wearing wires and he was in the kitchen with a cup of coffee and recording equipment. The recording couldn't be used in a court of law as it would also implicate Lincoln Brown and Ayesha, however Marsh was pretty damn sure that Harrington the Fourth would be more interested in protecting his own reputation.

Almost to the minute that they had predicted, the doorbell rang repeatedly. Someone was angry. Ayesha got to her feet, but no way was Marsh going to let her be the first in line. "I've got this."

He took his time getting to the door and then opened it slowly. Harrington the Fourth pushed past him. "Who the hell are you?"

"Marsh Adams. We met the other day, remember?" Marsh projected affability and cluelessness.

"Fuck you. Where is he?"

"Are you referring to Mr. Brown?"

Harrington ignored him, stomping toward the massive living room, his chest and head forward, his arms swinging at his side, like a bullet seeking a target. "What the hell did you do?" Harrington bellowed.

"Hello, Mr. Harrington. Can I get you a drink?" Ayesha said in her super-polite fake voice.

"You can get me my damn paintings."

"I'm sorry, I don't know you're talking about."

"You know exactly what I'm talking about," he hissed.

Lincoln Brown shuffled into the living room. "Jonathon? Marsh? What are you doing here?" He shot a confused look at Ayesha.

She mouthed, *trust me*. And stepped between her grandfather and the angry man.

So far Harrington hadn't said anything that would implicate him. Marsh hustled closer as Harrington got right up in Ayesha's personal space and started screaming at her. Spittle gathered at the side of his mouth and his face was an unnatural shade of red. "I want my Rembrandts."

"The only Rembrandts on Mr. Brown's schedule belonged to your father."

Lincoln dropped into the wing chair by the fire as if he was too weak to stand. Or as if he just figured out what Ayesha had done.

"Those are mine. You were supposed to steal the fakes."

"There are no fakes," Lincoln's voice shook.

"There damn well are forgeries. You know exactly what they are. You painted them." Harrington edged around Ayesha and stood over Lincoln Brown menacingly.

Brown shrank in his seat and shook his head. "I didn't paint any forgeries."

The conviction in his shaky voice was absolute. And Marsh realized...*he wasn't lying*.

Lincoln Brown wiped a trembling hand over his forehead.

"I'm sure the museum will be thrilled with your father's donation," Ayesha said.

But Marsh was stuck back on Lincoln Brown's words. He didn't paint the forgeries. Other little details came back to him. Prodigy. Genius. She practiced copying masterpieces. But that would have made her a child when she had painted the fakes.

"You know damn well you stole the originals and replace them with forgeries fifteen years ago."

"Are you saying that you commissioned forgeries and then replaced the originals in your father's house?" Ayesha asked.

Leading the witness. It would never stand up in a court of law. But that really didn't matter. That wasn't the objective here.

"Wasn't just me. Your grandfather isn't so lily white. You little bitch."

Ayesha's hazel eyes sparked but she didn't say a word. "So you're admitting that you commissioned forgeries and replaced the originals in your father's house with fakes."

"No one will believe that."

"It's a good thing we have a recording then, isn't it?"

Harrington headed toward Ayesha with his arms outstretched, as if he was going to strangle her.

Marsh blocked the older man, smacking down his arms.

"Don't you dare touch me."

"I don't think you're in any position to make demands," Marsh said. "It would be best if you saw yourself out."

"You aren't going to get away with this."

"We have a recording of your admission of guilt. It's up to you what happens next. But if you pursue this, I'm sure the authorities would be very interested to know that you paid someone to assault Ayesha Brown."

"You can't prove that," he bluffed.

"Turns out if you have a good enough hacker you can." Marsh smiled and it wasn't nice. "If I were you, I would cut your losses and be thankful that no one discovered that you stole from your own father years ago."

"I'm going to destroy you."

"If you try, you are going down too," Ayesha shot back.

"Not a problem, little girl."

Marsh stepped closer to Harrington. "Funny thing. We started investigating you when we discovered you were threatening Ms. Brown."

"Who the fuck cares?"

"Well now, that's a good question. I'm sure the SEC and the Federal authorities would be real interested in your offshore bank account in the Turks and Caicos."

Harrington whitened. "I don't know what you're talking about."

"They'd probably get a warrant to search all your accounts and your residences."

"You little shit."

"I bet they'd be real interested in the contents of your home—*all* the contents. Even hidden rooms are covered by warrants. You have some very nice artwork. Every facet of your life would come under scrutiny."

"You'd never get a warrant." He was still full of bravado and anger.

"Actually, I've got an in with a federal judge." And he would damn well use his relationship with his father to protect Ayesha and her grandfather.

Harrington deflated before their eyes. "Goddammit."

"You go after the Browns and I will make it my mission to destroy you." The menace in Marsh's voice scared even him.

Harrington swiped a trembling hand over his mouth. "You win."

"Good choice."

Harrington stormed out, defeated. Marsh watched him get in his vehicle and drive away. When he turned around, Ayesha was there. She threw herself into his arms and squeezed his waist tight. "Thank you," she murmured against his chest.

He wanted to wrap his arms around her and hold her. But she had lied to him, and she had put him in the position where he'd broken his word, yet again.

He kept his arms stiff, by his side and she realized quickly that he was not returning her embrace.

Viktor walked into the living room with the recording equipment and nodded at them. "Got it all."

Marsh said, "We will keep a copy of the recording for insurance purposes."

Ayesha stepped back and nodded, wiping away the moisture at the edges of her eyes. "Thank you. Is there… anything I can do?"

He didn't think she was talking about this situation. But just in case, he shook his head. "I'm done."

Chapter 17

Marsh was dreading this conversation with Jill.

He sat in her office on New Year's Eve. She'd been in Scotland for the past week. She looked well rested…and happy.

The same could not be said for him.

"I called an audible. There wasn't much time. If I didn't, ALIAS could have been implicated. But I've been trying to do better, be better."

"Marsh, I'm not mad. You also helped get us back on track. Did you see the Sunday section? The article is great."

"But we went from not wanting any publicity to being enmeshed in it."

"At least it's the good kind. And seriously, I'm working another angle as well."

"But—"

"Nothing. You didn't rush in and try to save the day by yourself. You used our team. Viktor and Jake were instrumental in getting shit done. And we did good. Ayesha is safe, her grandfather is safe, her show went off well, and the museum got their donation. It's a W."

But they'd used a lot of company resources to shadow Ayesha which was definitely an issue. "But money."

"The estate and the insurance company paid us extremely well to move those paintings." She fussed with the papers on her desk. "I think we should start contracting out some private protection."

Marsh considered the idea. "I miss those days."

"Me too." She hugged him. "How's Ayesha doing?"

"I wouldn't know. I haven't talked to her." And it was killing him slowly. But how did he forgive her? He'd had enough time to obsess over everything that had happened, and he understood to some extent that she'd been stuck. But she had used him.

"You are easygoing with everyone. Except your father. And now her."

"Yeah, well, she betrayed my trust," Marsh said. "And I just don't think I can forgive that."

She studied him for another moment. "You'll figure it out."

"Hey!" Kita blew into the room. "What are you doing here? Don't you need to get ready for the party?"

In a moment of weakness, he'd agreed to host the ALIAS New Year's Eve party at his place. What the hell had he been thinking?

AYESHA SHOULDN'T BE HERE.

She was technically crashing this party. She'd been trying to get in to see Jillian Larsen and the woman wasn't returning her phone calls. Until today, and she had said to come to this address tonight. All Ayesha could hope was that the rest of the ALIAS office, especially Marsh, hadn't arrived yet.

But she liked the symbolism of it. New Year's Eve. Closing out the old and ringing in the new. New beginnings with a clean slate.

The doorman buzzed her up with a smile.

She rode the elevator to the eighth floor. Even before she got off the elevator, she could hear the noise.

There were only two apartments on this floor. The door to 8B was propped open.

Shit. Her nerves jangled and she was tempted to turn around and leave. Except…she needed to do this.

She knocked on 8B but of course no one answered. The noise level was intense.

She looked around and shrugged, then pushed the door open.

The space seemed masculine, very spare lines and sleek furnishings. There was some interesting art on the walls. The owner had a good eye.

Ayesha scanned the partygoers, looking for her prey. And there Jillian Larsen was snuggled up with a white guy in the kitchen. They were smiling and flirting and so close together that the sexual tension between them created a force field keeping everyone else out.

Tough. She wasn't leaving until she talked to Marsh's partner.

She noticed several other ALIAS people all at once.

Kita, Viktor, and—was that one of the women who'd been at her show opening undercover? Ugh. She looked around, relieved not to see Marsh. The last thing she needed to do was run into him.

Her heart gave a pang. She missed him. She understood why he'd left. She'd lied to him. Put his relationship with his friends and business partner in jeopardy. She'd known that lying was going to screw him, and she'd done it anyway.

She'd have done anything to protect her Gramps, but she hated that she'd betrayed Marsh's trust.

She made a beeline for Jillian so she could say her piece and then get the hell out of here before Marsh showed up. She had no desire to make him uncomfortable. Based on the stares of the other ALIAS employees, some weren't real happy to see her either.

"Jillian."

"Well if it isn't the Artist of the Week."

Ayesha listened for sarcasm but didn't hear it.

"Hamish, this is the client I was telling you about." She introduced the hottie at her side.

"Pleased to meet ya'."

God, that accent. She'd bet no one was immune to him. Except her. She had no interest in a handsome Scot. She nodded and turned to Jillian. "Can we talk?"

"Come on in the guest room."

She wouldn't have pegged this place as Jillian's. It was too spare and too modern. But Ayesha was better with paints than people.

Jillian pulled the door closed. "What was so important that you called me exactly twenty times?"

Ayesha winced. Maybe she had gone overboard but this was important. "Don't penalize Marsh for my lies."

"You should have been honest with Marsh up front," Jill shot back, arms over her chest.

Ayesha snorted. "Right, because that's worked out so well for me in the past. I didn't know if I could trust him."

"A relationship based on lies has no chance of survival."

"Relationship? Oh no. It's not like that." Ayesha shook her head. "It was just…convenience."

Marsh burst into the bedroom. "What's wrong?"

"We were just talking," Jill said mildly.

He stepped in front of Ayesha. "She had her reasons, Jill."

He hadn't told anyone her secret. Her whole body relaxed.

"Don't judge her."

Jill raised an eyebrow and smiled. "I'm out. You should use Marsh's bedroom to talk this out."

"Marsh's…?"

"Oh, yeah, this is his place, not mine." Jillian waved her fingers and delivered a parting shot. "Don't fuck this up."

She seemed to be talking to both of them.

MARSH'S HEART was pounding harder than when he'd faced down a weapon from a violent mob enforcer back in his early days in the US Marshals. "What are you doing here?"

Ayesha closed her eyes and took a deep breath. "I didn't want Jillian to hold my behavior against you."

He'd been saving himself and everyone else since he was twelve. His first instinct was to refute her statement. "So you came here to stick up for me? To save me."

"Well, that was my intent." Ayesha took a step away from him.

"Why?" He was at a loss.

"No one has ever put me first." Ayesha wanted to pace but she held still. "You helped me when it was definitely not in your best interest to do so. You could have claimed ignorance and let me get caught." She glanced around, as if she was worried about listening devices. "Instead you went into that house with me."

Marsh's anger crumbled. He wanted to put her first all the time. The past week had been hell.

"Of course, if you hadn't followed me it wouldn't have been an issue."

Seriously? He wanted to laugh but he also wanted to clarify something. "I don't want your gratitude."

"It's not gratitude, you idiot."

Now he did laugh. "Tell me how you really feel."

"Didn't I just do that?" Ayesha snarked at him.

"You were willing to sacrifice everything for your grandfather even though he didn't look out for you." And Marsh loved her because she was able to rescue herself, but she let him help her. Holy shit, he loved her.

"Well, yeah. He's family."

"You forgave him."

"Well, I did realize that I had some unresolved anger toward him. But he's my Gramps. That one breach of trust didn't negate all the love and care he gave me before or after."

He still couldn't wrap his head around it. "How do *I* do that?"

Because he realized that he wanted to. He didn't think he'd ever completely get over what his father had done. But the only way he was going to move forward was if he granted forgiveness first.

"Acknowledge that everyone is human and flawed." She knew exactly who he was talking about. "Even your father. Me. You."

It sucked, but he had to do the work. Had to make himself vulnerable to get the prize. "So…you came to see me?"

She blinked. "Umm, no."

Shit. Maybe he'd read this all wrong.

Except…no guts, no glory. And he wanted the glory of her. With him. Every day. For the rest of his life, if she'd have him. "Come with me."

"Where are we going?"

He took her hand, marveling at the zing of electricity that arced through him. "I want you to see something."

"You're having a party. I should go." Her gesture toward the door was awkward.

"Not yet."

"Bossy."

"You know it."

Marsh led her into his bedroom, ignoring the king-size bed and turned her so she faced the picture hanging across from his bed where he could see it every night before he went to sleep. Regrets. Redemption.

"What…?" She whipped her head around to stare at him. "You bought it?"

"Of course I did. It's ours. A private moment between you and me."

"But no one knows that."

"I do." And he wanted to be the one who looked at that painting every day and remembered the night she painted it in front of him. "I wanted you with me every day."

"You probably could have done that without spending fifty grand."

"Only probably?"

"Maybe you can return it."

"Not a chance." He took a breath and leapt. "But I'd rather have the real thing with me to stare at every night before I go to bed and every morning after I wake."

He could see her heart pounding so hard, the hollow of her throat trembled.

"I could do that…if you're sure."

"The last week sucked." He wrapped his arms around her and tugged her against his chest.

"True story."

"Let's make a new story then." He bent his head and kissed her. She kissed him back. It was the perfect beginning to a new year.

Epilogue

ne month later

"ARE YOU READY?" Marsh whispered in her ear.

Ayesha's nerves jangled. "Maybe."

He wrapped his arms around her from behind and tucked his head into the curve of her neck. "I'm so proud of you."

Her heart swelled. The past month had been…amazing. After a week of deciding who was going to sleep where and figuring out the logistics of two households, she had moved in with Marsh. It was too soon. They both thought that, and yet they did it anyway.

She was painting during the day at her loft and going to his, *their*, place at night. The transition had been fairly easy. Although neither one of them cooked so they'd gotten one of those meal service boxes and they were learning together.

She turned around. "Confess. You're only attending because someone else is making dinner."

He snort laughed. "Fundraiser chicken is not the reason I'm coming tonight. I'm going to be there to support the amazingly talented—"

"And fabulously sexy," she interjected.

"—goes without saying," he kissed her behind her ear. "Sponsor of the Brown Scholarship for excellence in art."

Ugh. She hated being the center of attention.

"Hold on." He licked his thumb and rubbed it along her shoulder. "You had a little bit of paint."

She melted. "We could just stay home in bed."

"Nope." He twirled her around and skimmed his gaze over her body. Tonight she wore a bold red satin, strapless gown, with a long skirt and sharp stilettos. His gaze turned wicked. "Although I am curious about what's underneath that dress."

She laughed. "You'll have to wait and see." She may have bought something fancy for tonight. Because her lover was obsessed with her underwear.

MARSH FOLLOWED Ayesha into the festively decorated ballroom.

The fundraiser wasn't just about Ayesha's scholarship. The focus for tonight was to raise money for The Boys and Girls Clubs.

Crystal chandeliers glittered. The theme had something to do with art. The name tags were little palettes and the table decorations were paint cans with brushes and feathers in primary colors on white linen tablecloths. Volunteers wandered around with balloons in red, blue and yellow, offering a chance to pop for a prize.

"We're table one." She glided through the room with a

sexy confidence, but she stumbled a little when she got to the table.

"What's this?"

"I bought the table." His heart swelled with pride and not a little bit of joy. "Actually I bought two tables."

"Two? Who's going to sit at these?"

Everyone from ALIAS was coming. "Jill and Hamish, Kita and Alex, Maria and Dwayne, Jake, Zara." Those two would have to be separated. The normally unflappable Jake got extremely testy whenever their PR manager was around. "The only one who can't make it is Viktor."

Marsh frowned. Viktor still hadn't seemed to bounce back from what happened last fall. Marsh had tried to talk to him. He kept insisting that everything was okay, but it wasn't.

Ayesha flushed with pleasure. "You didn't have to do that."

"Everyone wanted to come." Truth but even if they didn't love fundraisers, they would have come to support her and Marsh anyway.

"Then who is at our table?"

"Hello!" His mother said from behind them.

Ayesha whirled around. "Colleen!" And her boyfriend, Harold, who didn't seem to be going anywhere. "Harold. So nice to see you."

His mom, dressed in a black sequined cocktail dress, hugged Ayesha and then Marsh.

"You look great, Mom." She did. She was glowing and he grudgingly admitted that Harold was good for her. It was still weird.

He looked over his mom's shoulder and there was the judge.

His mom said, as if she had eyes in the back of her head, "Your father and his latest…friend are with us."

Weirdly, his parents and the double date thing came to be. Marsh gripped the judge's hand for a manly shake but when his father pulled him in for a hug, he slapped him on the back. "Dad."

Baby steps. With Ayesha's urging, they had started getting together on Saturday mornings for hikes if the weather was nice enough and coffee if it wasn't.

He was slowly repairing his relationship with his father. Even though it wasn't perfect and he still had a lot of lingering resentment, he thanked God that his beautiful woman had shown him the way to forgiveness.

He hoped she would feel the same about him.

"Uncle Bobby." Ayesha hugged his dad and smiled warmly at his date, who was probably about Marsh's age. Surprise. The judge wasn't dating a teenager.

"Nice to meet you." Marsh shook the woman's hand.

"A pleasure," she said. "Your father is very proud of you." She smiled at the judge and her look held affection. Maybe his old man was learning.

"Thank you for com…." Ayesha stuttered to a halt, shock on her face.

He guessed his surprise was here.

Marsh turned to see Lincoln Brown headed their way. Beside him was a man who could only be Ayesha's father. "Surprise."

He could only hope it was a good one.

They'd had a lot of discussions over the last month about their complicated relationships with their parents. He knew that she regretted certain things about her teenage years. Maybe this was the wrong time, but the opportunity had presented itself and he'd jumped.

Her mother had declined the invitation to attend but she'd sent a note. Marsh opened it and read it. Still in protector mode, he would have destroyed it if there had been anything bad in it. The note had been polite but left the door open for future conversation. And it really did seem as if her mother had a commitment that she couldn't step away from.

The two Brown men reached their table.

"Hey girl." Her grandfather hugged her quickly. "Look who I brought."

"Dad?"

His parents and Lincoln faded away, but Marsh stayed put, stepping closer to protect her in case this was a monumentally bad idea.

"Ashii." Her father embraced her, closing his eyes and squeezing. He stepped back, his arms on her shoulders as he surveyed her. "You are looking well."

"What are you doing here?"

Good news. She didn't sound mad. More like confused.

"I am here to celebrate my daughter."

She looked over his shoulder.

"Your mother wanted to come but she had an official dinner that she could not avoid."

She shrugged. "It's no big deal."

"On the contrary. We are exceptionally proud of you." He pulled an envelope from his pocket and handed it to her. "As a matter of fact, we are matching your contribution so that there will be enough for two scholarships."

"How did you even know?"

"Your young man let us know that you were being honored."

Ayesha shot Marsh a look he couldn't interpret. His

heart was pounding harder than when he'd suggested they move in together and he began to sweat.

Now her father was reproachful. "You should have told us."

"You're busy."

"Not too busy for this. Clearly we failed to tell you how much we love you." He stepped back. "Perhaps we can talk more tomorrow."

"I'd…like that."

He nodded at Ayesha and then held out his hand to Marsh. "Thank you."

Marsh nodded once. "You're welcome, sir."

Her father melted away until it was just the two of them.

"I hope you aren't mad."

Her hazel eyes shone with love—at least that's what he hoped it was. "I should be. But I pushed you into reconciling with Uncle Bobby. It's only fair that you do the same for me."

Phew. Okay. She wasn't mad. "I did it because I love you," he blurted out.

"You…love me?"

"Uh, yeah."

"It's too soon."

Just like it was too soon when they moved in together. *When it's right you know.* "I've known since New Year's Eve."

"Seriously?" Ayesha put her hands on her hips. "And you picked this moment to tell me so? With two hundred people around watching us." She waved her hand at the crowded ballroom.

"I never said my timing was perfect." Marsh smiled. "As matter of fact, our timing has been all wrong from the beginning. But it doesn't matter. Because you're perfect for me."

The bell to sit for dinner was ringing.

"Here's some timing for you." She narrowed her eyes, leaned closer, and whispered in his ear, "I'm wearing a red lace bustier."

Marsh swallowed. She rarely wore underwear but when she did, he really, really appreciated it. After living with her for a few weeks he understood how much the fabrics irritated her skin. For her to wear lace was huge.

His body responded and he held back a groan. "That's low," he gutted out. There was no time to show her the other surprise for the night. He'd booked a suite at the hotel.

"Just so you know——"

The emcee was up on stage giving the welcome address as the attendees settled in their seats. "Please welcome, our keynote speaker…"

"——I love you too."

His heart expanded and all he wanted to do was grab her and take her upstairs.

"…Ayesha Brown," the emcee finished.

But that would have to wait. His woman had a speech to give and he couldn't be more proud.

The crowd clapped; the din from their friends and family was wild.

Just as she got up to speak, she murmured in his ear, "It's crotchless."

Well, damn.

WHAT'S GOING on with Viktor? Look for his story in Compromised, coming this Spring.

. . .

WHY DID the judge decide it was time to mend his relationship with Marsh and Colleen? Check out Stalked, book one in the ALIAS series, featuring rule follower, Alex Saunders, and rule breaker, Kita Kim…Click above to read about how they manage to co-exist (or not!).

THANK YOU, thank you, thank you for reading Marsh and Ayesha's story! I hope you enjoyed reading Deceived as much as I enjoyed writing it. If you did enjoy this novel, below are a few ways you can help a writer out!!

GOOD: Lend the book to a friend

Better: Recommend the book to your friends

Best: Leave a review at Amazon, BN, iBooks, Kobo, Google Play, Goodreads…basically any place they sell or review eBooks. Every review helps my work get out to other readers and I cannot even express how much it means to me when you let people know you liked my work. Readers have so many choices nowadays and limited dollars to spend. It can be difficult to take a chance on a new author even if the premise sounds appealing. By reviewing books, you give other readers insight into the story world and help them make informed purchases.

THANK YOU, thank you, thank you for your support!!

P.S. Would you like to know when my next book is available?

You can sign up for my newsletter at Lisa's Confidants I send out newsletters twice a month typically filled with info on upcoming books, friend freebies, and contests I'm involved in. I will never sell or distribute your email to other people.

Acknowledgments

Thank you to my editor Deb Nemeth for your patience and thoughtful edits. I am so grateful for your insight.

Huge thanks to my friend and writer Shannon Monroe for helping make sure that I got Ayesha right and didn't commit any egregious gaffes.

Thanks to Tawdra and Mel for the weekly convos about business and helping me stay on track. And thanks to Adrienne, Cecilia and Rachael for the monthly check ins from across the country. I miss you guys!

Thank you to Robin Ludwig of gobookcoverdesign.com for the beautiful cover.

Blessed to have you all in my life.

Cold as Stone (John, Family Stone #7)

Family Stone Box Set (Stone Cold Heart, Carved in Stone, Heart of Stone, Still the One, & Jar of Hearts)

The Nostradamus Prophecies

View To A Kill #1

Never Say Never #2

ALIAS

Stalked (ALIAS #1)

Hunted (ALIAS #2)

Vanished (ALIAS #3)

Billionaire Breakfast Club

His Semi-Charmed Life (Camp Firefly Falls #11 and Billionaire Breakfast Club #0)

Everything He Wants (Billionaire Breakfast Club #1 The Jock)

Queen of His Daydreams (Camp Firefly Falls #23 and Billionaire Breakfast Club #1.5)

Excerpt of Stalked

Excerpt of Stalked

Kita Kim took a direct hit across the chin.

Only the heavy padding saved her from a knockout blow. Her ears rang and white stars sparkled in her vision. That was what she got for letting her mind wander, even for a moment.

Kita shook off the daze. She was trying to train Hannah Smith to defend herself. The goal was to get Hannah to engage if one of her nieces was being attacked by their father. But if she hadn't fallen into that kick, it would have lacked the force needed to really hurt her.

Hannah got in a kick to Kita's thigh. She'd probably have a bruise, but the woman hadn't used near enough force to take down a two-hundred-fifty-pound man.

"Do it again. You have to kick hard enough to hurt a guy who weighs a lot more than you do." She purposely infused her voice with perkiness, leaving out the frustration.

Hannah nodded, setting her mouth and crouching into a defensive stance. Her eyes, lost in a sea of delicate, purpling skin, glowed with anger. Her muscles trembled with rage, but her matchstick arms would be no problem for the bulk and sheer power of her abusive brother-in-law bent on attack.

Unless Kita could get Hannah ready to defend against her attacker slash abuser slash brother-in-law, he would crush this woman, just as he had crushed Hannah's sister. At least, that was what they believed. Tammy Donner had disappeared. After a cursory investigation by the local police, Frank Donner had been cleared. He insisted that his wife had run away and left him and their three daughters.

But Hannah and Kita knew the truth. Frank Donner had killed his wife. And if Kita couldn't get Hannah to defend herself and her nieces, she was worried he would kill Hannah too.

Somehow Kita had to get Hannah to embrace her rage. Whip her into a vengeance frenzy. Or at the very least, induce her to not curl up into a defensive ball.

Because Kita's boss, Jillian Larsen, had refused to help Hannah. Even though Hannah Smith and her nieces were just the type of clients usually helped by the agency Jillian had cofounded.

Adams-Larsen Inc. and Associates—publicly an exclusive PR firm—was privately a relocation specialist agency.

"We don't break the law," Jillian had said to Kita emphatically.

Because Adams-Larsen, or ALIAS, as she and her coworkers affectionately called it, skated on the edges of legality. While nothing they did was outright illegal, there were definitely blurred lines. At the end of the day, they saved people. And Kita loved being part of justice for those wronged.

Which is why this situation sucked big hairy donkey balls. Hannah Smith was in serious trouble.

Frustration bubbled in Kita's stomach. She hated when abusers picked on someone weaker. *Asshole.*

She could take down the brother-in-law with ease. But Frank Donner wasn't going after her. And Kita could only offer Hannah lessons while she wasn't on a case. If Kita received a new assignment, she'd have to cut back on training Hannah.

Kita held up her arm and rubbed her nose through the concealing face mask.

Jeez, she was ripe. The earthy odor of sweat steamed in the padded assailant suit. Her powder scent deodorant, which had worn off an hour ago, left her less than fresh. Major body odor wafted into her nose along with the unhealthy scent of Hannah Smith's fear.

Normally Kita reveled in this type of workout but Hannah's obvious discomfort hit at Kita's consciousness and her muscles were rigid with impotent frustration. Tension ratcheted up with every sobbing breath Hannah took. The threat to Hannah was real and immediate, not some faceless, nameless bogeyman, but a man who had and could kill. Even if no one but Hannah and Kita believed it. But Jillian Larsen didn't care that Kita believed Frank Donner was a killer.

"Kita." Jill had gentled her voice. "I understand your aversion to authority. It's a good part of the reason we hired you. I even understand your frustration."

Kita had rubbed at the abnormal bump on her wrist, the break that hadn't quite set properly when she was seventeen.

Jillian didn't always play by the rules either, but she couldn't understand something she'd never experienced.

Kita knew in her improperly-healed, ached-when-it-rained wrist that Hannah Smith was in mortal danger.

Adams-Larsen had the means and the contacts to save Hannah and her three nieces. But they weren't going to.

"Again." Kita prepped to attack the slight woman.

The bulky padding made Kita look like the Michelin Man on steroids. Due to years of training, she could move with a fair amount of agility, probably more than Hannah's brother-in-law possessed. But Hannah needed to learn to counter the violent threat. She needed to work past her fear and get angry.

Kita rushed Hannah, roaring, trying to scare her, trying to shake her.

Within seconds Hannah leapt out of Kita's path, then twirled with a roundhouse kick to Kita's back. Kita rolled, then swept Hannah's feet out from underneath her, and she hit the padded floor with a thud. Kita jumped to her feet and leaned over her.

The woman lay on the mat, her eyes closed, her cheeks gaunt and the yellowed bruising, from the black eye before this one, apparent in the bright florescent lighting.

"You okay?"

Hannah's chest heaved. Through the entire training session she hadn't said a word. Not once had she cried out, even when Kita had struck a blow.

A single tear trailed down the side of Hannah's face and pooled in her ear. Kita's heart shattered at the defeat pulsing off this woman in waves.

"How am I ever going to do this?" Hannah's voice shook and she still hadn't opened her eyes.

Kita refused to give up.

"Right now is when you strike," Kita said fiercely.

"Right now, with your heavy booted foot, you kick as hard as you can at his crotch."

Sweat poured down Kita's back, and her hair matted to her skull underneath the face mask and extra padding.

"Kick me as hard as you can," Kita demanded. "Don't hesitate. You won't hurt me." The crotch had been reinforced to protect the suit wearers, usually men, from the debilitating blows.

"You're so strong," Hannah whispered. "You don't understand how hard this is."

A heavy, gaping crater swallowed Kita's heart. Air stuck in her throat, and her lungs resisted her breath so sharply the gasp hurt. She grasped Hannah's shoulders. She hadn't always been strong. And she knew exactly how fucking hard this was for Hannah.

"You do not have to be a victim."

Hannah whimpered. Kita knew she wasn't hurting the woman, she was barely holding on to her.

"I can't do this."

"You *can.*"

Kita wanted to rage at the system that let a violent offender go free to terrorize his family, the very people he should protect and keep safe.

But she knew, better than anyone, that life wasn't always fair. And the only one you could count on to protect you—was you.

For a moment she wished Marsh Adams—her friend, her mentor, the man who'd showed her these moves when she'd been facing her own demons—was here. As Jillian's partner, Marsh was the reason Kita worked for the agency. But Marsh was MIA these days, out on assignment, and no amount of wishing was going to bring him back.

"You can do this." Kita leaned forward in a lunge,

holding out her hand, waiting for Hannah to grasp it so she could pull the tiny woman to her feet.

"He's going to kill me." The defeated slump of Hannah's shoulders sparked a resounding denial. No way was she going to let Hannah's asshole brother-in-law win. She'd do whatever it took to make sure Hannah and the children were safe.

"Not if I have anything to say about it."

The rumble of the employee garage door vibrated through the gym floor and the protective mats, shimmying up Kita's body to stop in the region of her heart. Adrenaline flooded her. It was the middle of the morning and as far as she knew everyone at the office was accounted for.

Except Marsh.

But ever since an incident in this building last month, the staff had been a little on edge.

Could just be someone in the field coming in for tech or ops help. Although she didn't have any appointments on her calendar. Could it be Dwayne or Victor, coming back from a relo early?

The first set of locks disengaged. Then the second door lock buzzed, the click resoundingly loud in the sudden silence of the sparring room. Hannah cowered on the floor as Kita shifted to watch the mirrors lining the wall and to observe who entered the facility.

A transparent bullet-resistant wall, made of layers of glass and polycarbonate, isolated Kita and Hannah from any threat in the hallway. The only way into the sparring room was through the password-protected entrance to the locker room on the other side of the building. The basement had been revamped to accommodate the sparring room, showers, lockers and the totally indulgent steam room.

Hannah grabbed her hand and Kita hefted her up to standing with one forceful jerk. "Again."

Kita split her attention between Hannah and the mirrors.

Hannah smoothed down the material of her yoga pants and dropped back into a defensive stance. Kita nodded in approval. *Yeah, that's it. Kick my ass.*

The steel-reinforced door opened slowly. The shadows beyond the entrance to the garage were dark and somehow ominous. Her tension ramped up as she readied to attack Hannah, while her brain shifted into higher gear, preparing to defend Hannah against danger. Which was stupid because whoever was coming through the door would have already had to go through several security checkpoints before being allowed access to the building. Adams-Larsen took their security seriously. No one who didn't belong breached the facility.

No one.

And since the shooting last month, security had been tighter than ever.

Kita's heart thumped loudly in her chest. *The ba-bump, ba-bump* a rapid percussion, as her hearing preternaturally heightened while she waited for whatever, whoever, was coming.

A silver-haired man with broad shoulders and an imperious bearing—something about his demeanor so arrogant the very air around him seemed to be holding its breath—stepped through the door. The single halogen light illuminated his face with startling clarity. She'd never officially met him, but, she knew who he was. She'd seen pictures in Marsh's office.

The judge. Marsh's father.

In the shadows behind him another man paused in the

doorway. Ignoring the workout room and sparring women, the judge strode down the hallway like he owned the place.

Hannah kicked out and Kita twisted carefully to block the kick to her thigh. "You need to hit right on the knee."

Hannah nodded and crouched again.

Something in the movement of the second man drew her gaze back as he entered. He pulled the reinforced door closed behind him. The overhead halogen beam highlighted the almost blue-black of his hair and emphasized his broad shoulders. He kept his face turned away from the observation windows, staying in the shadows.

Not Marsh. It had been stupid to hope that Marsh was coming. It had been what felt like forever since he'd been in the office.

Apprehension shivered over Kita's spine. Hannah shifted so she was slightly behind Kita.

Ironic. Both the man above her and the woman behind her were hiding.

For a moment, the man paused. He had stepped into the light, head tilted down, watching the defensive tableau, his pale blue eyes piercing, glowing with intensity. Kita felt the man's regard like an almost physical caress. Her visceral reaction to the quick assessment was confusing, unwanted.

As if a rush of pheromones had drop-loaded into her system and made a beeline toward her female parts.

Her five-ten body was cocooned in the padded assailant suit, her breasts smashed and wrapped to protect from blows, and her ombre blond ponytail encased in the watch cap underneath a large padded helmet. Sex should be the last thing on her mind.

With an instant dismissal he followed the judge to the waiting elevator.

Why her hormones, which had been dormant for a very,

very long time, suddenly stood up and started howling was a mystery. But the damn things were banging on the door, demanding to be let in.

Ridiculous.

"Who was that?" Hannah asked softly.

"No one we need to worry about." Kita shook the unexpected reaction to the stranger out of her head. She curled her fingers at Hannah in a "bring it on" gesture. "Kick me again."

Hannah kicked out at Kita's padded hands in a one-two-three pattern.

But there was no power behind Hannah's attack. Her moves were still timid, unsteady.

"Try to *hurt* me." Kita kept her tone firm.

But Hannah continued to be lackluster rather than aggressive.

"I just don't know if I can do this." Her shoulders slumped, her gaze dropping to the padded floor. "What if he wins?" she whispered.

"We won't let him win," Kita said fiercely. Her blood pumped in a river of anxiety but she kept her demeanor fierce.

Because she truly believed that if Hannah Smith didn't either learn to defend herself or, better yet, disappear with those kids, they would all be dead soon.

Excerpt of Stone Cold Heart

Excerpt of Stone Cold Heart

Family Stone #1 Jess

In the early evening dusk, Jess Stone lay on her stomach in the twenty foot high rubble of a demolished church, underneath a black and gray city-scape tarp intended to camouflage her position. A sharp-edged chunk of debris dug into her lower rib cage, the scope of the Remington M24 cool and familiar against her face.

Her standard uniform of jeans, running shoes, and plain black t-shirt rendered her just another anonymous and transient relief worker...which she was actually. A black baseball cap hid her distinctive multi-hued blonde hair. The paper mask kept out the contaminated dust from the destroyed buildings but did little to stem the overwhelming stench of decaying bodies.

Tanks rumbled through the destroyed coastal town, their public address system blasting warnings for citizens to stay in their homes, curfew was in effect. The threat was a joke.

Ninety percent of the people in the town didn't have homes left. Those who did were terrified to go back inside. In the fetid, humidity choked air, the tent cities erected in the parks and on the beach were seething masses of the injured and shock struck.

The substandard construction in the small country had never been enough to withstand the angry might of Mother Nature. Buildings had toppled like a stack of Tinkertoys, and left crumbling cement walls with twisted rebar poking out of the jagged ruins like a skeletal hand.

Trapped in the concrete pieces that littered the ground, the heat from the tropical day seared through her thin sturdy clothing. The stank of the raw sewage that ran in rivulets through the streets overpowered the salt-laden breeze off the ocean. People, covered with the grit of pulverized buildings and humans, shuffled along with blank vacant stares. Two weeks after the quake, still in shock, their lives decimated first by nature and then kicked and beaten by the ineffectiveness of a flawed relief system. Hundreds of humanitarian agencies had descended on the population duplicating efforts and yet completely missing the need in other areas. The government was ostensibly trying to coordinate the effort, however the mass chaos was undeniable.

Through the Leupold Ultra M3 fixed power sight, she tracked the movements of Henri LeRoy, leader of this tiny island nation, violator of human rights and dignity, and all around poor excuse for a human being.

Sickness roiled in her stomach. The power bar she'd eaten for breakfast threatened to add to the rubble pile as she tried to figure out how in the hell she'd ended up here. Back behind a sniper rifle with the power over life and death trembling in the muscles of her right trigger finger.

Dammit. When she'd decided to take control of her life and quit the FBI, she hadn't wanted to do this anymore.

She'd wanted to be a simple relief worker. She'd wanted to connect with her family, brothers and mother.

But that bitch, fate, had slapped her upside the head and now here she was, where she'd sworn she never wanted to be again. Looking through the scope of a high-powered rifle, with a crystal clear head shot and a murky sense of right and wrong.

With little fanfare, she could blast LeRoy's brain matter all over the silk-covered walls and the antique Louis the XIV scrolled chairs in the receiving room of his ridiculously elegant weekend mansion which, since built properly, had sustained minimal damage. Her muscles twitched with the knowledge and acceptance that with one slow slide of her finger, the despotic, amoral leader would be history.

Jess didn't want to kill him, didn't want to be directly responsible for another death. She didn't want this choice. She'd given up this kind of life. She'd left the FBI after a series of high stress cases to get away from the doubt and guilt that had crippled her. To make her own decisions about right and wrong rather than carry out the commands of her bosses.

But if Henri LeRoy lived, chances were astronomical that many other citizens would die.

And yeah, she'd probably been manipulated into this. Actually no probably about it. Assassination had not been listed as one of her duties when she'd joined Global Humanitarian Relief. Damn her brother anyway.

But now all she could do was lay here in the desecrated remains of the former church and hope that her special skill set wouldn't be needed.

Fortunately, she was secondary backup.

And unless several things went horribly wrong, she would break down her weapon, get back to the relief aid encampment, back to actually helping people, and be out of here without ever firing her rifle.

Then she could hand out seed packets to her heart's content and figure out what she was going to do next. If she'd stay with GHR and her brothers, or go. First, she had to get through the next two hours.

But if something did go wrong...she prayed that if she was called upon, she could make the right decision. Make the shot. Cold zero.

About Lisa

USA Today Bestselling Author Lisa Hughey started writing romance in the fourth grade. That particular story involved a prince and an engagement. Now, she writes about strong heroines who are perfectly capable of rescuing themselves and the heroes who love both their strength and their vulnerability. She pens romances of all types—suspense, paranormal, and contemporary—but at their heart, all her books celebrate the power of love.

She lives in Cape Ann Massachusetts with her fabulously supportive husband and one somewhat grumpy cat.

Beach walks, hiking, and traveling are her favorite ways to pass the time when she isn't plotting new ways to get her characters to fall in love.

Facebook

Instagram

Pinterest

Twitter

Bookbub

www.lisahughey.com

Lisa's Confidants

* 9 7 8 1 9 5 0 3 5 9 0 7 3 *